THE HALF-TRUE LIES OF CRICKET COHEN

BOOKS BY CATHERINE LLOYD BURNS

. . . . . .

The Good, the Bad & the Beagle

The Half-True Lies of Cricket Cohen

For adults

It Hit Me like a Ton of Bricks:
A Memoir of a Mother and Daughter

THE HALF-TRUE LIES

OF

CRICKET COHEN

......

CATHERINE LLOYD BURNS

Farrar Straus Giroux · New York

Farrar Straus Giroux Books for Young Readers
An imprint of Macmillan Publishing Group, LLC
175 Fifth Avenue, New York, NY 10010

Copyright © 2017 by Catherine Lloyd Burns
Printed in the United States of America by LSC Communications, Harrisonburg, Virginia
Designed by Elizabeth H. Clark
First edition, 2017
1 3 5 7 9 10 8 6 4 2

mackids.com

Library of Congress Cataloging-in-Publication Data

Names: Burns, Catherine Lloyd, author.
Title: The half-true lies of Cricket Cohen / Catherine Lloyd Burns.
Description: New York : Farrar Straus Giroux, 2017. | Summary: In trouble at home and
  school again for turning in a not-quite honest memoir, eleven-year-old Cricket and her equally
  fanciful grandmother, Dodo, set out on a crosstown Manhattan adventure.
Identifiers: LCCN 2017018549 (print) | LCCN 2016038539 (ebook) |
  ISBN 9780374300418 (hardback) | ISBN 9780374300425 (ebook)
Subjects: | CYAC: Imagination—Fiction. | Grandmothers—Fiction. | Old age—Fiction. |
  Schools—Fiction. | Family life—New York (State)—New York—Fiction. | New York (N.Y.)—
  Fiction. | Humorous stories. | BISAC: JUVENILE FICTION / Family / Parents. |
  JUVENILE FICTION / Humorous Stories. | JUVENILE FICTION / School & Education. |
  JUVENILE FICTION / Social Issues / Friendship.
Classification: LCC PZ7.B9364 Hal 2014 (ebook) | LCC PZ7.B9364 (print) | DDC [Fic]—dc23
LC record available at https://lccn.loc.gov/2017018549

Our books may be purchased in bulk for promotional, educational, or business use. Please
contact your local bookseller or the Macmillan Corporate and Premium Sales Department at
(800) 221-7945 ext. 5442 or by e-mail at MacmillanSpecialMarkets@macmillan.com.

For my mother

THE HALF-TRUE LIES

OF

CRICKET COHEN

1

IF ONLY SOMETHING WOULD
FALL OUT OF THE SKY

Cricket Cohen was dreading summer vacation. Her mother, Bunny Cohen, had signed her up for surfing camp with Lana Dean. Cricket would rather swallow a big ball of snot than do anything with Lana Dean. Lana Dean had very long and curly eyelashes and she acted like having long and curly eyelashes was something to be envied the world over, like her being born with them was a giant accomplishment. But Lana Dean had nothing to do with her eyelashes. Eyelashes were genetic. And Cricket had no interest in surfing. She didn't want to skim the surface of the ocean, because all the interesting, important stuff was deep down, way down underwater.

Cricket was rarely interested in what other people were interested in. That's why she was usually alone in the school yard during recess, thinking about stars. About how instead of twinkling, twinkling in the sky like in the lullaby, stars actually pelted the infant earth like bombs. They exploded, shrapnel flying everywhere, lava flowing like water. Gas and flames covered the ground she sat on right now. The whole planet was on fire. In such an inhospitable world, Cricket wanted to know, why did life start?

She knew *how*. The flames died and the temperature dropped and oxygen and hydrogen found each other and formed water. After that, life was inevitable. Single-celled shapes swam around and multiple-celled organisms joined the march and here we are today: society, the human race, middle school, summer vacation in two days, and surfing camp with Lana Dean.

But why? What gave life the big idea to give it a go?

This she could not figure out.

A fast-moving object swiped through her peripheral vision. Cricket's heart raced. A meteor! Something worthwhile was happening. Finally, and she was in the right place at the right time. For once.

But it was just a softball.

Typical.

Vincent Lee and Sara Paul, the team captains of the softball game taking place in the center of the school yard, looked over. Cricket detected the usual worry in their eyes. Like they couldn't predict what crazy thing she would do with their stupid softball. Cricket may have been odd, but come on, she knew what to do with a ball. She picked it up and threw it at them. Vincent and Sara ducked and then seemed relieved. Cricket sat back down and drew an amoeba on the concrete with a pebble.

The origin of life was, without a doubt, the most interesting thing in the world to think about. Which was why no one in her sixth-grade class thought about it at all. All they cared about was organized sports or being popular. What was wrong with the youth of today? Maybe she was too hard on them. Maybe she shouldn't sell them short. Some of the kids in her class were more advanced and were able to care about both sports and being popular. At the same time.

Cricket longed for the olden days of lower school, when recess in nearby Central Park was the best period of the day. When after read-aloud the teacher brought out the rope with the loops and you held on. The teacher looked out for trouble so you didn't have to. The teacher said when to cross the street, when there was dog poop or stranger danger, and when it was time to let go of your loop and play.

Cricket and Veronica Morgan had always held opposite loops because they were best friends. They climbed the rocks. They had a jewelry store. They collected treasures. They worked in a coal mine. They were astronauts. They lived in a castle.

Vincent Lee yelled, "Safe!" and suddenly everyone was yelling and arguing and Cricket had to wonder when playing—when life, for that matter—had gotten so strict and so boring. The rules and the nets and the bats, the bases and the goals, the penalties, the different-shaped regulation-size balls. Oh, forget it.

Cricket liked games where she made up the rules. That's why she usually stood in the center of the playground waiting for an asteroid to hit her on the head or near the chain-link fence pretending to be in a prison-break movie digging a hole to freedom with a plastic cafeteria spork.

Lana Dean and Juliet Lysander and Heidi Keefe made their third loop around the yard. For reasons Cricket would never understand, walking in a circle while talking was what popular people who weren't sporty did during recess. Cricket would be bored out of her mind walking around in circles. But she had to admit Lana and Juliet and Heidi looked like they were deep in a good conversation. It was almost tempting to join them. But knowing the limits of their intellects, they were probably talking about socks.

Here's the thing. In her humble opinion, Cricket could, if she wanted to, be popular. But being popular meant you liked what other people liked, and that wasn't for her. Cricket was the outlier. And she didn't care. Except she did, a little, because there was no one at school to talk to. Who could she tell what she had heard the astrophysicist say last night on the radio? That if you added up every single sound and word ever made by a person, the number you'd get would be much smaller than the number of planets in the universe. That was an idea worth contemplating. Infinity. Let's face it— infinity was an idea you could think about forever.

Cricket's best friend, Veronica Morgan, was a person with deep thoughts. But she'd gone to a different school last year and Cricket hardly ever saw her. Now Cricket's ideas and the imagination that imagined them were her only friends. No one else trusted imagination anymore.

2

CRICKET AND DODO PLAY A TRICK

Cricket walked home along Columbus Avenue, pondering the last two school days before the beginning of dreaded summer vacation and trying to distract herself with what to buy for dinner. Her mom, Bunny Cohen, was a renowned fund-raiser and list maker. She was also a terrible cook. That's why she often gave her daughter a shopping list of prepared foods to buy at Bilson's.

Bilson's was a market on the Upper West Side that had survived the Depression. It had also survived, according to her father, World War II, the lefty-liberal days, the young-stockbroker days, the single-room-occupancy days, the families-with-hypoallergenic-dogs days, and was still standing as foreign bankers bought up apartments that they didn't even live in. Cricket didn't know what all this meant, but she did know that a lot of people her family knew were moving to Brooklyn because housing prices in Manhattan were too steep. But Brooklyn wasn't exactly a bargain. One day, Richard Cohen said, Queens would be the new Manhattan. Cricket's father liked reading the *New York Times* and making grand predictions. Everything, he said, even gentrification, was a cycle that went round and round, repeating itself in some form or other.

As Cricket approached Bilson's, she recognized the hulking form of Abby standing guard outside the entrance. Abby was probably the only person in the world Cricket would be able to identify without her glasses on. Because Abby was basically the size of a tree. If you cut her open she'd probably have two hundred rings inside. Abby was the latest woman hired to take care of Cricket's grandmother, Dodo Fabricant.

"Hi, Abby," Cricket said.

"She won't let me inside," Abby said, clearly frustrated.

It was her job to accompany Dodo on errands, but Dodo Fabricant didn't want Abby. Dodo didn't want a handler.

"She told me to wait," Abby said.

She was not amused, but Cricket was. Her grandmother Dodo Fabricant was tiny, and the idea that she could make Abby, who was so enormous, do anything was funny.

"She wants to pretend to be shopping alone," Abby said. "She made me walk behind her. All the way here. Your grandmother . . ."

Abby didn't finish the sentence and Cricket thought that best. Cricket didn't like when Abby said less-than-positive things about her grandmother.

The Cohens had a charge account at Bilson's, which meant Cricket could go in anytime and get whatever Bunny told her to. She grabbed a cart and started shopping. Abby may have been mad about waiting outside, but the truth was that Abby probably couldn't fit through the narrow aisles inside Bilson's without knocking everything over. The original Mr. Bilson must have been very small. The place was designed for small people. Even though the store had expanded over the years, the aisles hadn't been widened in the process. They were original. The tiles behind the butcher counter were also original. So was the potato-salad recipe, for that matter.

It was from 1927, and was framed behind the butcher counter in Mr. Bilson's wife's handwriting. The current butcher was the third cousin once removed of the original butcher. There was still a fishmonger, a bakery, and the famous counter with prepared foods. Cricket took a deep breath, because the smell of Bilson's rotisserie chicken was one of the best smells in the world. It was the only thing that could compete with Dodo's roast chicken.

Dodo had taught her granddaughter the art of chicken roasting. They used to pretend they had a cooking show on PBS. They made it very professional. Everything they did they demonstrated and narrated for the home audience, and all their ingredients were measured out ahead of time in little glass bowls on the counter. First, Dodo washed and dried the chicken. Then Cricket sprinkled the inside with salt and pepper. Dodo made Cricket shove her arm really deep into the chicken. Next, Dodo rolled a lemon back and forth on the counter to loosen up its juices. Cricket poked holes in the lemon with a fork. Dodo and Cricket stuffed the chicken with the lemon, a bunch of smashed garlic cloves, and a handful of fresh thyme and rosemary. Then they rubbed the outside of the chicken with softened butter and Cricket put lots more salt and pepper all over the skin. Then Dodo did something magical. She carefully tucked herbs under the skin of the chicken and, as the chicken cooked, the herbs flavored the meat. The chicken roasted in the oven on top of a pile of roughly chopped onions and carrots and turnips. Dodo left the oven light on so Cricket could watch the juices from the chicken baste the vegetables. Dodo's roast chicken was The Best.

In another episode, Dodo taught Cricket how to make an omelet in the style of Julia Child. She said that if Cricket could roast a chicken properly, prepare an omelet, and make a decent vinaigrette, she'd be able to take care of herself. Dodo was a big fan of independence.

Cricket's ringtone chimed. She jumped.

"Hi, Mom."

"Cricket?" Bunny asked.

"Yes, Mom, who else would I be?" Bunny always sounded a bit suspicious when Cricket answered her phone, as though it might not be Cricket.

"Where are you?"

"At Bilson's."

"Oh my goodness. I thought you'd been kidnapped. Are you almost done?" Bunny asked.

"I just got here," Cricket said. She'd come right after school. She didn't know what her mother was all wigged out about.

"Well, please don't forget the rotisserie chicken."

"Mom, are you serious? That is the main reason I came here!" Bunny had no faith in her. She hung up and, just to annoy her mother, walked past the rotisserie chickens and straight to the ice-cream freezer.

She stared through the cloud of condensation. Her glasses fogged up almost immediately and it was hard to read the flavors. She took them off and wiped them with her T-shirt. Butterscotch Pudding and Salted Dark Chocolate sounded good, so she put both in her cart. When she looped back to the butcher counter, she found her grandmother holding a basket with a jar of mustard in it. Nothing else.

Dodo was talking to the butcher. She was wearing her signature outfit: a trench coat, sunglasses, and a French silk scarf. She looked like a spy from the Cold War. Or an actress playing one. Dodo always reminded Cricket of an old film star. Dodo loved old movies.

"Billy," she said, "I can't eat a whole chicken. What else is good?"

"Everything is good!" Billy exclaimed. "What about a lamb chop? I got a gorgeous lamb chop!"

Billy had the loudest voice Cricket had ever heard. She wondered what he sounded like when he was angry. He'd probably blow a roof off.

"A what chop?"

"I said, a lamb chop."

"A veal chop?"

"What?"

"Billy, I asked you, what's fresh?"

"Are you being fresh with me?" Billy said.

Dodo and Billy were about the same age and it was cute how much they liked each other.

"Hi, Dodo!" Cricket said.

Dodo turned around, flustered. "Poopsie!"

Dodo grasped Cricket by both cheeks. She loved those cheeks. "What's the hot gossip? What's new?"

"Well, I'm shopping for dinner."

"So am I, isn't that right, Billy?"

"What's that?" he said, pulling on his left ear as if that would make his hearing better.

"I said, isn't that right?"

"Isn't what right?" Billy said.

"Dodo," Cricket said, "you're coming to our house for dinner. You are one of the people I'm shopping for."

"I am?"

"It's Monday. You always come for dinner on Monday."

"Of course I do. I thought it was Tuesday. Never mind. We used to play bridge on Tuesday, remember?"

"I loved bridge night!" Cricket said. Dodo used to live in California, and Cricket visited. All of Dodo's friends were loud and opinionated and funny. Cricket would lie on the yellow couch listening, soaking it all up. Sometimes she'd sit next to Dodo and try to learn the game. Bridge was a game you played with candy in little dishes. Dodo put small glass bowls of bridge mix everywhere for the Tuesday-night games. Cricket's family never had dishes of candy anywhere. And they never played games. Bunny and Richard Cohen claimed they didn't have the patience for games.

"Hey," Billy said. "What about me? Your grand-daughter shows up and I'm chopped liver. I knew you were out of my league."

"Billy, if you're chopped liver, then I'm toast. We go very well together. But I'll see you tomorrow. I have din-ner plans with my granddaughter."

Abby was standing right outside where Dodo had left her.

"All right, Mrs. Fabricant," she said. "Let's go. Will you hold on to my arm?"

"No," Dodo said, "I will not."

Cricket laughed and got a dirty look from Abby. Abby acted like Dodo was in her protective custody and Dodo acted like Abby was nuts. "My grand-daughter will take me. Abby, you can go home now."

"Mrs. Fabricant, my shift is not over and I am not going home."

"Abby, I don't want you. My daughter is the one who wants you. Please show a little respect. I am a grown woman."

"If your daughter wants me, there must be a reason," Abby said.

"There is a reason. You're quite right. The reason is that she is controlling."

"Abby," Cricket said, "I'll walk her."

"And I will walk behind you," Abby said. "But I'm not going home."

"Oh! I forgot mustard. Abby, will you please go in and pick me up a jar of Dijon mustard?"

"Yes," Abby said, lumbering inside. As soon as the doors closed behind her, Dodo said, "Let's make a run for it!"

The light was hard and bright and Cricket wished she had a pair of sunglasses, like Dodo. They were escaping, after all; they should both be incognito.

"What's the gossip, Poopsie?" Dodo said.

"School is over in two days."

"That's good, isn't it?"

"Yes. Except Mom signed me up for surfing camp. I don't want to go to surfing camp. I want to go to geology camp or at least science camp. It's so dumb I have to get up at the crack of dawn for two weeks during my vacation to do something I don't want to do."

"Your mother is very bossy. I don't want Abby. She signed me up for that. I didn't want to live in New York, but she made me do that, too. I was perfectly happy with my own life in California," Dodo said.

Cricket had been happy when Dodo moved to New York City a year and a half ago. She liked having Dodo right down the hall. She wished Dodo were happy about it.

"Remember when we used to have adventures?" Dodo said. "I want to take you somewhere. To Paris. I want to see you."

"You're seeing me tonight. You're coming to dinner, remember?"

"Dinner, yes. But I mean an adventure. Remember when we used to have adventures? We used to tell stories. Remember?"

"Mrs. Fabricant!" Abby screamed from down the block. "I see you!"

"Quick, let's make a run for it!" Dodo said.

3
RECESS REVISITED

The next day the sporty kids divided up into teams while Cricket recovered her contraband spork. She had stolen it from the cafeteria and wrapped it in a napkin and hidden it under some plants. That was very authentic. If she were in prison planning an escape, that was what she'd do. Occasionally some of the other kids looked over at her.

She wished they'd quit looking and help her. It was hard to dig a secret escape tunnel through the sunbaked dirt under the chain-link fence. Her spork barely had any prongs left.

Usually in a prison break you had a little help from another inmate. But no one in this prison wanted to get out.

She was surprised to discover that Lana and Juliet and Heidi had mixed things up today. They were walking counterclockwise. They were such rebels.

The truth was, Cricket could be judgmental. Plus she and Lana were about to be surfing buddies. Maybe Lana and her amazing eyelashes weren't as vain and annoying as Cricket thought. She decided to abandon her scraping and join the girls on their loop around the playground. She felt like a hobo jumping a freight train.

When Cricket hooked her arm with Lana's, Lana was surprised, but she didn't stop walking. So far, so good. Cricket gave Vincent Lee the dirtiest look possible, but he didn't see. It turned out Lana and Juliet and Heidi were not talking about socks. They weren't talking at all. They were singing.

"Hey, I want you again, I'm so sure," Lana sang, quietly and slightly off-key. Poor Lana—apart from her eyelashes, she really didn't bring much to the table.

"Hold me, baby, count to ten," Juliet sang more vigorously.

Cricket knew the song. Everyone in the world did. The girls were singing the latest number-one hit from the world's most popular boy band. The band had a reality show on the Internet. The kind of reality that was super scripted. The kind of reality based on a pretend version of life. In the show the band members were best friends and each week they struggled and triumphed, writing their own material and somehow just scraping together the rent. In real life, Cricket guessed, they probably didn't like one another, write their own material, or know how to play any instruments, and they were almost certainly very, very rich.

"You're my cure, darling, no one else, but anything you want, I'm sure," Heidi sang with passion.

Now it was Cricket's turn.

"Babe, I did it again," Cricket sang. *"I pooped on the floor, wipe it up, close the door. Help me, I'm so insecure."*

Juliet and Lana laughed.

But Heidi shrieked and held her sides. "I'm going to pee! Cricket, you are so hilarious."

Cricket adored Heidi. Maybe Juliet and Lana and Heidi were the nicest people after all? Maybe surf camp would be okay. Maybe Cricket had finally figured out recess. Maybe she'd made friends and wasn't a loser after all. Maybe you could be popular *and* have fun.

"I'm going to the concert. My parents bought me tickets for my report card," Juliet said.

"We haven't gotten our report cards yet," Heidi said. "We don't get them till tomorrow, on the last day."

"I know, but they always get me something at the end of the year," Juliet said.

"But how do they know you deserve it?" Lana said.

"I deserve it," Juliet said.

Heidi rolled her eyes.

"I'm dying. And so jealous, Juliet," Lana said, batting her eyelashes.

"You are? Lana, you're the one going to private school next year."

"No, you're so lucky, Juliet," Lana moaned.

"Do you even understand?" Heidi said.

"I'm going to make a really big sign that says I LOVE YOU, LINCOLN, because if your sign is really big and they notice, you can get picked for a meet and greet. With them."

"Oh my gawd," Heidi said.

"I can't even. You guys, they are everything," Lana said. "Juliet, you have to be chosen and take their picture, and tell me every single syllable that happens."

"I promise, Lana. I swear."

"You guys," Cricket said. It had been a while since she'd contributed and she wanted to make it count. "My father is their lawyer."

"Shut the front drawer," Lana said.

Cricket could feel her new friends' excitement. She upped the ante.

"His caseload is mostly corporate real estate, but they put him in charge of the band because he went to high school with their manager."

"Oh my gawd," Heidi said. Her mouth stayed open, but nothing else came out. Lana and Juliet were grinning from ear to ear.

Cricket's new friends loved her story. She had to keep the good times coming. "They came for dinner last night," Cricket said.

"No," Juliet said. "You did not just say that."

"Oh my gawd."

"Wait," Lana said. "Cricket, you always lie. You're lying. She's lying. You're a liar, Cricket Cohen. I should have known."

"Ever since kindergarten. When you lied about that accident. I bet you never even had stitches," Juliet said.

"I heard you didn't even fall off any rock. You staged the whole thing with ketchup," Heidi said.

"I did so fall off that rock. What are you talking about? Who carries ketchup around? I had forty-nine stitches. My head cracked open."

"So you say," Lana said.

"I bet those glasses are fake. You're a human lie ge-nome," Juliet said, and the three of them walked away.

Cricket was stunned. Stunned that they had left and stunned by how much it hurt. It hurt way more than the volleyball that had hit her in the head three weeks ago in gym. She had to find her way back to the spork fence. She needed something to hold on to. Making up words to a song you didn't like was fine. Saying that your father was the lawyer for the singers of that song was fine. Saying that he had gone to high school with their manager was fine. But saying that the band had come over for dinner, that part was not fine. She'd ob-viously said it to help them because walking in circles was boring. She hadn't done it to be mean. She'd done it to be nice. She didn't care about any dumb boy band. Lana and Juliet and Heidi lied all the time when girls called them on catty things they'd said. *They* were not nice. *They* were mean. Really mean. Tears burned like acid behind her eyes, but she refused to cry. Even if it meant going blind.

4
WATCHING THE CLOCK

At three o'clock, Cricket's classmates would be released into the wild. But she had a meeting with her parents and Mr. Ludgate instead. Cricket stared at the unmoving clock. It was going to be 2:50 forever.

Maybe being stuck in last period for eternity was better than the impending meeting. A meeting with the teacher and your parents was never a good thing. But then an exciting idea occurred to Cricket. Maybe she wasn't in trouble. Maybe Mr. Ludgate had called the meeting because he had decided that Cricket was too smart and interesting for middle school. He was sending her straight to NASA to begin her time as chief astrophysicist to the ambassador of Iceland. This was a farewell meeting.

She doodled fjords and swirling constellations all over her margins. Life in other countries and on other planets had to be better than life here.

Lana Dean reached behind herself and handed Cricket a stack of summer reading lists.

Cricket could barely look at her. Surfing camp was going to be impossible. Cricket's existence was torturous, but she took a list and passed the stack.

Why did all the books for kids her age have characters dying of cancer? It was so boring. Not the death part. Death was exciting. Something was happening, you were dying! But the cancer? Couldn't authors come up with another life-threatening condition besides cancer?

Lana fluttered her eyelashes. What if Lana was diagnosed with cancer? She'd have chemo and all her eyelashes would fall out.

Cricket felt a nudge. There was another stack of papers to pass down. She took a sheet without looking. She felt horrible for wishing Lana would get cancer. She drew hearts all over both papers to make up for it.

The bell rang and a landslide of kids tumbled past Cricket and out the door.

When the classroom had emptied, Mr. Ludgate looked up from his papers. "Cricket," he said, "I need to straighten out my desk. I'll meet you in the library in five minutes."

Mr. Ludgate's blotter was centered and all his pens and paper clips and staples were lined up, each in their own glass jar, next to a big ball of rubber bands. Cricket had no idea what Mr. Ludgate could possibly make straighter, but she took her backpack and left for the library.

5

BEARS AND SQUIRRELS
AND HOT-AIR BALLOONS

The library was on the top floor and had a skylight. When it rained, the raindrops made little pinging sounds against the roof and it was relaxing. Maybe after she was an explorer-astrophysicist she would be a writer and she would visit school libraries. But not today. She dreaded going there today. Her parents were always so stressed in meetings with teachers. Actually they were always stressed-out, but they were more stressed-out in meetings with teachers.

What if she couldn't walk? What if her parents hadn't vaccinated her and she had been stricken with polio? If she had polio she'd never make it up these endless stairs. Her legs would be too stiff from illness to bend. No wonder she played alone with a spork in recess while the other children ran and were athletic. She was a poor polio patient. How would she get up all these stairs? In the olden days someone would have carried her. But this was now and there was no one here.

She looked at her poor, withered legs. So sad. With all her courage she took a tremendously deep breath. Cricket Cohen, polio victim, tried lifting one leg over the other. She gripped the banister with all her might, knowing she'd have to hoist herself up, hopping. But she didn't have the strength. She couldn't pull her dead legs up and over a single step. She was perspiring. She was probably breaking into a fever. She'd never make it.

She surrendered and walked up the stairs like the fully vaccinated person she was.

Her parents, of course, were already in the library. They were never late, anywhere, ever. Richard Cohen looked uncomfortable sitting in his child-size chair. Bunny Cohen rested her head on her husband's shoulder. She was wearing her usual assortment of off-white clothing, which she fondly referred to as *buff.* Every hair was in place. But she was crying.

"Cricket," Bunny said, giving her daughter a damp peck on the cheek and sniffling.

"Hi, honey," Richard said.

Cricket handed her mother a box of Kleenex. She gave her father an abbreviated kiss.

"Thank you, honey," Bunny said, wiping her eyes with a tissue. "Abby and my mother had another fight. No one I hire can stand working for Dodo. Not that I blame them, the whole situation is a disaster. But don't worry. I promise I will pull myself together when your teacher walks in. He won't know a thing."

Abby, Abby, Abby. She always threatened to quit.

"Poor Bunny," Richard said. He was comforting his wife like she was a six-year-old.

Cricket ran her hand across the laminate-topped table, which was pale blue. Everything about the library, except the presence of her parents, was soothing. The posters on the walls were some of Cricket's favorite images. The two bears in beds made of logs covered by complementary patchwork quilts shared a nightstand piled high with books. *Reading gives us a place to go when we have to stay here*, the caption said. Another poster featured a family of squirrels climbing aboard a hot-air balloon. *Fly away with books*, that caption said.

I wish, thought Cricket. How ironic that her mother was responsible for the library. Before Bunny got on the PTA the school didn't even have one.

If only Cricket were boarding a hot-air balloon right now. Or turning into a squirrel. Ha! If she were a squirrel, she would be the kind with a really good tail. Not like the ones with the thin, gross tails that looked like reproductive experiments between squirrels and rats. Those squirrels were horrifying.

When Mr. Ludgate arrived, Cricket wondered if he'd not only straightened his desk, but had also pressed his clothes. He shook hands with her parents. Just like Bunny had promised, her eyes were dry and she was all smiles.

The sun streaming through the skylight above Mr. Ludgate made his neck red. It glowed and Cricket could sort of see plasma in there.

"Thank you for coming in," Mr. Ludgate said as he sat down.

He had something stuck in his teeth. If he knew, he would die.

"What I'd like us to talk about is—"

"The way our daughter bends the truth?" Richard said, glancing at his wife.

Cricket looked at her father incredulously. Bunny made sure to look straight ahead. Had Lana and her squad reported Cricket saying the boy band was a client of her father's?

"Let's not get ahead of ourselves," said Mr. Ludgate. He put his papers in two piles. Sometimes Mr. Ludgate was boring, but Cricket forgave him because he was fond of her. He'd said her final memoir was so interesting he'd actually sent a copy to Dr. T, the geologist whose blog Cricket followed. Cricket had never written to Dr. T, but it was her dream that Dr. T would recognize Cricket's geological passion and invite her on a field trip.

It turned out, though, that while Dr. T told Mr. Ludgate she was supportive of Cricket's interest in geology, she also told Mr. Ludgate she didn't know anyone named Cricket Cohen and had never traveled with an eleven-year-old to Iceland to observe rift valleys, but the descriptions of the trip were uncannily familiar. Mr. Ludgate explained this was why he'd felt it necessary to call a meeting.

"I don't want this to be a character assassination," he said, trying to smile reassuringly. "But, Cricket, you didn't complete the memoir assignment as intended. Furthermore, the experiences you described were both fabricated and borrowed. You made up a story about accompanying Dr. T on her adventure, and you lifted descriptions of those adventures from Dr. T's own writings. Isn't that right?"

Cricket wished she could climb under the covers with one of those bears.

"Mr. Ludgate is asking you a question, Cricket," Richard said.

"Cricket, answer Mr. Ludgate," Bunny said.

Whenever Bunny found things unpleasant she got extra-bossy.

"What?" Cricket asked.

"Mr. Ludgate is speaking," Bunny said.

"I was saying that you didn't exactly hand in the memoir I assigned, and it was hard to give you a grade on it."

"I did hand it in."

"Mr. Ludgate says you didn't. Either you did or you didn't," Richard said.

"Cricket," Mr. Ludgate said, "the criterion for memoir is writing that is based on the truth."

"Divergent plates are true," Cricket said.

"Cricket, I don't doubt your passion regarding geology."

"Cricket, I don't understand your obsession with rocks," Bunny said. "I never have," she added, smiling.

"You've never been to Iceland. Alone or with any Dr. T!" her father declared as though he were the only person with a firm hold of the facts. He reached for a Kleenex and wiped his brow. "Plagiarism is against the law. Do you understand how wrong this is, young lady?" Richard asked. He took these things very seriously. He was a tax lawyer. He had studied the law.

"Well, Cricket hasn't committed plagiarism, per se," Mr. Ludgate said. "She hasn't copied Dr. T's words and pretended they were her own. She's only imagined sharing certain experiences with the scientist."

"That's true, Richard," Bunny said.

Cricket wasn't interested in any of this. She was interested in plate tectonics.

Plate tectonics theorizes that the earth's continents rest mostly on seven major plates located on the outermost layer of the planet, called the crust. The crust is rigid. But the slabs spread apart and come together. They are shifting all the time. Pangaea broke apart because of movement at plate boundaries. The continents are still moving. Just like cells in the human body replace themselves every seven years on average, the earth's topography and geology redefine themselves every several million years. Science, the most fact-based, dependable thing we have, accepts constant change as reality.

But it was frustrating that so many dramatic things happened so slowly. Or that they happened so far away they might as well be invisible. Ninety percent of plate spreading, for example, occurs along the ocean floor. Underwater volcanic eruptions had created a mountain range more than forty thousand miles long. Cricket was dying to explore it.

Some of her favorite images were photos and videos of lava erupting undersea and cooling instantly in the water, solidifying into billowy puffs. Cricket wanted to watch that in person. She wanted to swim alongside the Mid-Atlantic Ridge and see all the rare jellyfish and the sea worms that burrow in the rocks and the strange undiscovered glowing fish that light up in those dark depths. The government spends more money on space exploration than on deep-sea exploration, so not that many people have been down there to explore. There is one place on earth, however, where two huge plates are spreading above water. That place is Iceland, and that was what Cricket had written her paper about.

"Did you go to Iceland?" Richard Cohen asked for the second time.

"What?" Cricket asked. Her father knew perfectly well she had never been to Iceland. He also knew she would give anything to go to Iceland. If she were capable of going anywhere by herself to pursue the things that interested her, she would. But she was a kid, and kids weren't allowed to do anything. She'd already been on all the geological walks through Central Park that the Museum of Natural History had to offer.

So, like the posters in the library had been advising her to do since kindergarten, Cricket had boarded a hot-air balloon in her mind and traveled to Iceland. She'd written the adventure she wanted to have. It didn't hurt anyone and she was sure her memoir was more interesting than anyone else's, too.

"Oh, Cricket. Why must you make everything so complicated?" Bunny said. "Either you went to Iceland or you didn't. Things are or they aren't."

Bunny liked order and structure and dependability. Cricket liked creativity. Maybe she'd been adopted. Or switched at birth. Except she was a lot like Dodo and Dodo was Bunny's mother, so probably not.

This meeting was like a trial. Cricket was being treated like a criminal. Her parents and her teacher were the prosecuting attorneys. What a story. And the cameras, so many cameras! Everyone from the press was taking her picture over and over. *Click, click, flash, flash.* It was blinding. She needed sunglasses, something to shield her eyes.

What would this jury of book-loving bears and thrill-seeking squirrels find more important? Factual truth or the ideas and the story? Couldn't everyone involved just focus on the things that Cricket thought were important?

"Mr. Ludgate," she began, in her own defense. "You said the seed had to come from inside. Rocks excite me."

"You were doing great, Cricket. Until the part about Dr. T. And being the youngest geologist traveling with her. And the detailed description of standing in Iceland with one foot on either plate."

Cricket's opinion of Mr. Ludgate plummeted. Those were the best parts of her memoir. Standing still while the very ground beneath her feet was moving, literally transforming—that was amazing. Cricket liked to imagine standing across the rift, one foot on each side. One day, the rift between the plates might get so deep, visitors would have to pick a plate to stand on. One slab or the other.

"What I wrote is real. People have been there. Just not me," Cricket said. "But I wish it was me. I wish I had stood there."

"Cricket, you could have written your memoir about your passion; that would have been absolutely appropriate. It's that you wrote a memoir about a trip that you never went on. You made the whole thing up," Mr. Ludgate said.

"Cricket, the shortest distance between two points is a straight line. Why do you always take the twisted, convoluted, unpaved road?" Richard asked.

Cricket bit her nail. She was going down. And so young. "So Much Promise: The Cricket Cohen Story." Now that was a good title for a memoir.

"It's more scenic?" Cricket offered. She was seeing all those spinning newspapers used in black-and-white films to indicate events unfolding. When the papers stopped spinning, the headline was revealed: *Cricket Cohen, Eleven-Year-Old Heroine, Rescued by Her Own Wit and Good Heart. Verdict: Innocent!*

"The purpose of memoir," Mr. Ludgate said, "is to reveal, through stories of your own life, the larger truth about life for your readers." He spoke very slowly so there was no chance of misunderstanding.

"I wasn't telling lies," Cricket protested.

"They are half-truths at best," Bunny said.

"Cricket, I admire your enthusiasm and imagination very much. You've been one of my most engaged, interesting students all year. So I kept your grade what it's been the rest of the year. But I'd like you to redo the assignment. Try not to think of this as a punishment but as an opportunity."

Cricket stared at him in disbelief. He could call it whatever he liked. But homework over the summer was a punishment.

"Write about a personal experience that somehow transformed your awareness. Just make sure *you* are the person who changes. Don't mess with the facts. You're an excellent writer. You don't need to pretend to be someone you're not. I know you can do this," Mr. Ludgate said, looking deeply into Cricket's eyes.

"Wait, grades are already in?" If grades were in, why was he making her redo this? What was the motivation?

"Yes, they are," Mr. Ludgate said. "I gave you the grade you would have gotten if you'd followed the directions and done the work you usually do. But I'm letting you rewrite this assignment. Hand in your rewrite by Monday. I'll be here, cleaning out the classroom and so forth. This is on the honor system. I'm trusting you."

"This is a big responsibility," Richard said.

"Don't disappoint Mr. Ludgate," Bunny said.

Case closed. Court adjourned. Her parents shook hands with her teacher. Her teacher tried to hug her. The defendant, Cricket Cohen, was sentenced to rewriting her memoir following the same prompts and rules as everyone else. In other words: no made-up imagined stuff.

She went home with the prosecutor and his wife.

6

ABBY'S THREAT

Abby was waiting outside the front door of the Cohens' apartment.

"Your mother is hiding again," she said.

"From you?" Bunny asked, trying to feign amusement. But the way she manhandled the lock on the door, nearly breaking the key, spoke volumes.

"Start at the beginning, Abby," Richard said. Cricket put her backpack on the Cricket Backpack Peg that her mother had hung in the foyer next to the hat rack. There was a place for everything on the tight ship Bunny called home.

"You know I am very good at my job," Abby said. "You hired me based on my references. In my business all I have are my references and my gratuities."

"Yes, Abby. You had excellent references," Bunny said, smoothing her blouse.

"But normally you don't lose your clients, do you?" Richard said with a smile.

Cricket laughed.

"Richard! You're not helping. Neither are you, Cricket," Bunny said. She led everyone into the living room. Abby sat on one sofa and Bunny and Richard and Cricket squished themselves onto the love seat opposite.

"I'm needed but not wanted," Abby said.

"You are needed, and I want you," Richard said, and immediately winced. "Bunny, help me."

"Abby, you are needed and you are wanted," Bunny said. "My mother doesn't know it yet, but she will."

"She is a very independent woman, your mother," Abby said. "I'm not sure this is going to work out."

"Please, Abby. I know it hasn't been the easiest transition . . . And I know that's putting it mildly. But I am fund-raising the whole of August and planning for the gala every day before then. I don't think I can do a single thing well if I'm worrying about my mother at the same time."

"My references are excellent. You know that the last family I worked for, they took very good care of me."

"Yes, Abby, you're a treasure," Bunny said.

"If I may," Richard said. "What about the location of Dodo right now? Is that not a concern?"

"She's probably in the basement," Cricket said.

"The basement?" Bunny asked.

"She brings a book or the *New Yorker*. She doesn't like the programs Abby watches on the TV and she doesn't like the sound of the TV on all the time. She said it makes her feel like she's in an institution."

"Cricket! That is not a nice thing to say," Bunny said.

It was true, however. Those were Dodo's exact words.

"I have impeccable references," Abby reminded them.

Cricket didn't like Abby, but Abby was right. Dodo was an independent woman. This plan, someone checking up on Dodo, might not work out.

7

SHE'S LOSING IT

Cricket was sent to the basement to retrieve Dodo, who was in fact sitting in the laundry room with the latest issue of *Art Forum*. Cricket brought Dodo to her apartment before returning home. In the Cohen kitchen, her father was trying to engage her mother in a conversation that Bunny was doing her best to prevent.

"Bun, your mother."

"Richard, please," Bunny said. "I don't care to discuss it."

"She's losing it."

"Richard. I assure you, my mother is not losing it. I just the other day had a lengthy conversation with her about the Matisse cutouts. You don't know her. She's never had patience for things that don't interest her. And guess what? Old age doesn't interest her. Leaving California and living in New York City doesn't interest her. Going to the dentist doesn't interest her. I do not interest her. That's why she doesn't show up for lunch with me. It's why she doesn't pay attention to the calendar. I love the calendar, so she thinks it is ridiculous. Fun times." Bunny rewrote her mother's dentist appointment very neatly on the calendar. But no one loved the calendar as much as Bunny did because Bunny was the only person in the world who felt truly free within the confines of a rigid schedule.

"Cricket, did you find Dodo?"

"Yes, she was reading downstairs."

"Good. Now let's talk about your mother. I mean your memoir. Are you ready to start your memoir? I don't want Mr. Ludgate to regret his decision."

If the assignment were Bunny's, she would have finished it in the elevator while bringing Dodo back upstairs. Bunny believed in running headfirst at things that needed to be done. Bunny liked to impale herself on the task at hand.

That's why Bunny Cohen was the best fund-raiser Cricket's school had ever had. Aside from redoing the library, she'd started a program with the Whitney Museum, and one with the High Line park, just to name a few. But more important than just having the idea for these programs, Bunny had raised the money to pay for them. It is hard for anyone to say no to ideas that are ready to go and fully paid for. Bunny's fund-raising and the programs she paid for with her fund-raising had made Cricket's public school one of the most sought-after in the city.

Bunny had been very proud to support the New York City public school system until she heard a story on the radio that got her fired up about how New York's supposedly diverse public schools were terribly segregated by race and family income, far more than Bunny had ever realized. This meant that as fabulous as Cricket's school in her well-to-do neighborhood was, there was another public school in a nearby poor neighborhood providing very little for the children enrolled there. If you went to public school in a poor neighborhood, chances were the school was falling apart and needed teachers and resources as basic as chairs. The report said those schools offered advanced-placement classes composed of a single worksheet and then free time the rest of the period because the teacher lacked the materials to teach. Bunny had sat in her kitchen that day shaking her head, saddened and embarrassed to find out that public education was what she called "just another form of government-sponsored oppression." When would the world stop letting her down? She was enraged. When would separate but equal actually end?

She quit the PTA of Cricket's school and Richard quit his job as partner of the law firm. The Enrichment for the Public Fund was born. They decided to level the playing field and they became champions for the New York City public school system in a way that had not been done before.

They fund-raised money and they personally put music and dance programs, partnerships with museums, green roofs, food gardens, trips to Philadelphia, and art programs in every school in every neighborhood that needed them. Their motto was "Put the Public Back in Public Education." Their plan was to make every school great and every neighborhood desirable. If the school board wouldn't take on segregation, Bunny and Richard would give it a try. Cricket knew the whole spiel backward and forward. They'd drilled it into her since she was seven years old. This summer their goal was to raise five million dollars in a single night. Last summer they'd raised three million.

Bunny always said the closer she was to the money the more money she could raise. That was why they lived a lifestyle they couldn't afford. And that was why the Cohens always rented a summer house in the Hamptons after the season had started. People who hadn't rented their houses yet were desperate and took a lot less money. Last summer the Cohens had rented a house that was featured in a home decor magazine. It was furnished entirely in white leather. They got it for next to nothing. But they'd had a horrible summer because Bunny wouldn't let anyone eat or drink anything inside the house—God forbid something spilled and the owner kept their deposit.

The telephone on the wall rang and Cricket ran to answer it.

"Cohen Family, how may I direct your call?"

Sometimes Cricket liked to answer the phone like she was an employee. It irritated her parents.

"Hi, Milaya, hold on," Cricket said. "Mom, it's Milaya."

"Hello," Bunny said. "Oh no! Milaya, I'm so sorry.

Is there anything we can do? Milaya, stop. You have to take care of your mother. I understand," Bunny said, and hung up.

"Well, crisis number two has arrived. Milaya can't babysit the night we go to the Hamptons to find a house. Her mother is in the hospital."

"I don't need a babysitter," Cricket said. "I don't like Milaya babysitting."

"Don't be silly," Bunny said, carefully erasing Milaya from the calendar. "You love Milaya."

"I did before. But not now. She stays in the room with me until I'm sleeping. I hate it. I can stay by myself. It's one night. Dodo is down the hall. I used to have sleepovers with her all the time in California."

Bunny appeared to consider it and then seemed too overwhelmed to consider it at all. "Cricket, please go write that memoir. Two pages. Mr. Ludgate is counting on you. You gave him your word. Don't let him down."

The Cohen family was at an impasse. Dodo didn't want Abby. Cricket didn't want to write her memoir or learn how to surf. She didn't want Milaya to babysit, and Milaya couldn't come anyway. Richard wanted his wife to admit her mother was crazy. And Bunny didn't care what anyone wanted.

8

ESCAPE TO THE PARK

Cricket got her report card the next day. As promised, Mr. Ludgate had given her an excellent grade in spite of her owing him a paper. She had written a memoir about things that never happened. That was called lying. But Mr. Ludgate had given her a grade based on work she hadn't completed. That was called decency. Her parents wanted her to behave responsibly and not let him down. The pressure of life was too much.

What if nothing in her life ever changed? What if after she left home and began college and lived her own life, she just kept disappointing new people for the same old reasons? What if her whole entire life turned out to be an epic story of wasted promise? That was a good title for a memoir. She'd better remember that.

The last day of school always felt like a waste of time. Cricket was relieved when it was time to head home. Except she realized the first thing Bunny would ask her would be if she'd written her memoir. As though Cricket had been goofing off all day, procrastinating, instead of being at school, where she'd been forced to waste precious time.

Cricket hugged the stone wall along Central Park West and let her backpack scrape against the soot-covered rocks. Her mother would be furious. The wall ran the entire length of the park: from Fifty-Ninth Street all the way up to 110th Street. It was the most unassuming wall imaginable. But behind it was relief from anything that ailed you. Cricket entered through a break between Sixty-Fourth and Sixty-Fifth Streets. She wasn't ready to deal with her mother. The Japanese tree lilacs were in full bloom. Cricket loved how Central Park had more than two hundred species of flora.

In the olden days, if you were a city person who wanted to blow off steam in a natural setting, the only public places with flowers and trees in America were cemeteries. Public parks were only a reality in Europe. Last year Cricket had done a group project about Central Park. The group got an A even though Heidi Keefe and Sam Tremay were lazy. All they'd wanted to do was get images off the Internet and put them in a Power-Point. That wasn't interesting enough for Cricket, so she had done all the work.

And she'd learned so much. For instance, the location of Central Park was chosen because the land between Fifty-Ninth Street and 110th Street was rocky and swampy and not good for building on. Too bad for the Irish pig farmers and the German gardeners and the free African Americans who lived in a thriving village on the same patch of land. Cricket felt guilty loving Central Park as much as she did, considering how many people had been displaced to make room for its construction. But as her parents liked to say, fund-raising and changing the world were complicated.

Something else Cricket had learned was that Frederick Law Olmsted and Calvert Vaux, the designers of the park, were more than just landscapers. They were engineers, too. Olmsted designed a series of hidden roadways and bridges for vehicles and separate walking paths and tunnels for people. One of the best things about being in the park was feeling like you'd escaped into the wilderness.

The park had been created for all people, regardless of economic status, race, or background. But public transportation didn't exist in 1876, when the park opened. So the only people with access to it were the rich citizens of Manhattan who lived nearby or could afford a carriage ride, and so the primary purpose of the park—to be a welcoming place for all people—was not achieved.

The creators made another well-intentioned mistake. The enormous park began to decline almost immediately. They forgot to make plans for upkeep. By the 1970s Central Park was a dismal, run-down, drug- and crime-ridden shadow of its former self.

Now, thanks in large part to Bunny's friend Carolyn Petty, who was the president of the Central Park Conservancy, the park thrived. Cricket had spent her whole life sharing America's first European-style park with birdwatchers, joggers, children, families, painters and their easels, tourists with maps and cameras, people reading, dogs, and many others. But her favorite park companions were the rocks. Central Park was a geological museum.

Umpire Rock, in the southern end of the park, was a piece of Manhattan Schist with a set of man-made steps in the middle, but Cricket never used them. She liked climbing. The view at the top was great. Hotels to the south; apartment buildings, including hers, to the west. The zoo, the carousel, and Fifth Avenue, where Veronica Morgan lived, to the east. Looking north: the ball field, Belvedere Castle, and the Sheep Meadow.

Those were the obvious things to look at from the top of Umpire Rock. But as a geologist, Cricket examined the rocks. That was what a geologist was, a rock doctor. And over time the rocks revealed so many secrets. They told you all their stories.

Umpire Rock had been a patient of Cricket's for years. The solid mass she was sitting on had started its life hundreds of millions of years ago as sand and sediment covered by water. During infancy, the sand was exposed to tremendous pressure. The pressure turned the sediment into shale. In childhood, more pressure and heat turned the shale into schist.

Umpire Rock spent its adolescence being crushed, pulverized, pressurized, and heated even more. It buckled and folded. Crystals formed underground and became what we call Manhattan Schist, the bedrock of Manhattan.

The rock's young adulthood was spent under ice a thousand feet thick. Sediment and trees and boulders were dragged by glaciers across Manhattan. Umpire Rock had deep grooves that looked like claw marks made by a giant animal. Scars left by the Wisconsin Ice Sheet. Every rock had an interesting life story if you knew how to read its marks.

Cricket loved thinking about the way the world was before she was in it. Sometimes she sat on Umpire Rock imagining dinosaurs wandering around where she was sitting. Central Park was full of ginkgo trees, and dinosaurs loved ginkgo leaves. Dino footprints had been discovered just up the Hudson River Valley from New York City. Dinosaurs totally could have been here in Manhattan.

Even though rocks told you when and how they were formed, they might not be able to tell you the whole story. The Wisconsin Ice Sheet, for example, left evidence of its presence for geologists and explorers to find. But it also vandalized parts of what came before, because as a glacier travels across land, the debris it drags along transforms what is below, sometimes erasing older evidence. True, dinosaur fossils hadn't been found in Central Park. But dinosaur tracks had been found near New Haven, Connecticut. Maybe dinosaurs were here but the Wisconsin Ice Sheet erased the proof.

Maybe Cricket would be the geologist who discovered a clue about the New York City dinosaurs. Maybe she'd team up with a paleontologist. Maybe they'd fall in love and discover all kinds of incredibly important fossil evidence. Cricket adored science because the more scientists figured out, the more there was to know. That was the point in science—to keep going. Her parents liked to tell her that things *were* or they *were not*. But rocks were living proof that life was lots of things, sometimes all at once.

"Cricket Cohen," a familiar voice called up.

9

VERONICA!

Veronica Morgan and a little dog were looking up from the ground, smiling.

"Young lady," Veronica said. "You're too high."

Veronica and Cricket had shared so many experiences together, so many days and nights and years together, that Veronica could transport Cricket to another place and time. She was a human time machine. Cricket was now back in first grade again, being chastised by Ms. Whitman, a teacher who didn't approve when Cricket and Veronica refused to play with the other children. On their class's frequent field trips to the park, Ms. Whitman always scolded Cricket for climbing too high on these dangerous rocks.

Back then it was Veronica's job to stay on a relatively flat section of the rock, about midway up, which they'd designated their shop. Veronica organized the merchandise in their Central Park jewelry store, and Cricket's job was to collect mica and quartz and hopefully the odd emerald. It was demanding work, but Cricket was an explorer, so she didn't mind. The rule that Ms. Whitman tried to enforce was that no one climb higher than the teacher's head. But Ms. Whitman was very short and Cricket was goal oriented even then, which meant that every day she wanted to climb a little bit higher than the day before. Something might be up there—a bald eagle or maybe the other side of the world—and she needed to see it. Plus the emeralds. There obviously weren't going to be any emeralds low down. That would be too easy. The emeralds had to be way high up, out of the way.

Cricket was a good climber. She used whatever rock she was scaling like a ladder, wedging one foot in a crack, gaining purchase with her hands, and then advancing a bit. She set little markers for herself along the way so she could track her altitude. Veronica never climbed. She hated to get in trouble so much that she always followed rules. Veronica was afraid of falling. Cricket was not afraid of falling. Even that would count as an adventure. And she was an adventurer.

The day that Cricket did fall, there was a lot of blood. Cricket would never forget it because Andy Gregg had always told everyone they were ignorant about the true color of blood. He said blood was blue. He said veins were blue because that was the color of real blood. Well, Cricket's blood was red and the amount of it made Ms. Whitman nearly pass out. Mr. Littleton, the principal, had to come. Mr. Littleton scooped Cricket into his arms and carried her out of the park all the way to an emergency clinic near Columbus Circle. Cricket knew that she and Mr. Littleton would marry when she was old enough and he would always come to her rescue. Bunny met them at the clinic. She ran thirteen blocks, in high heels.

For Cricket, it had been a great day. The blood, the romance, the doctor who sewed up her head like an old shoe, the stitches, the bandage, the way everyone was scared of her the next day at school. She'd had to get forty-nine stitches in her little-girl head. She was made of tough stuff. She was awesome.

"Hello, old friend," Veronica said, carrying the dog up the stairs in the middle of Umpire Rock. She was still the cautious one.

"Wait," Veronica said when she was about halfway up, "is your mom here?"

"No, she's home with the air-conditioning on and the windows closed. Who's your new friend?"

"Claude." Veronica lifted one of Claude's paws and made him wave. His big paw looked out of proportion to the rest of his body.

"Claude is cute. And a careful climber, like his mother. Are you his mother?"

"Hmm. I'm kind of his sister. Or his aunt? It's a long story. Remember that necklace we shoved in here? Where did it go?" Veronica asked. She rummaged around in the cracks, poking them with a little twig, hoping to find it.

"I guess the pirates came."

"Those were some mad pirate days. We were lucky to escape without being kidnapped. We were lucky your mom didn't kill us."

"Swashbuckling was not her idea of age-appropriate play."

"Poor Bunny."

"Poor Bunny? Why?"

"It's hard to be worried about your daughter all the time, Cricket."

"My mom is always thinking about the children of

the public school system. Believe me, she isn't thinking about me. Ever."

"Oh, Cricket. You always think people don't like you. You know what my parents, the ever-so-inappropriate psychiatrists, think? They think your mom blames me for you falling off that rock and getting seventeen stitches in your head."

"Forty-nine."

"Cricket, tell the truth."

"My head was really little. Seventeen stitches in my head then would probably be like sixty-one stitches now. And I'm rounding down. Wait, Cadbury had puppies?" This dog was much littler than Veronica's other dog, which she'd seen at the park one day.

"Well, it's a long story and even Cadbury doesn't know," Veronica said. "This is Cadbury's son."

"Are you serious? How old was he? It's weird how early animals can have families."

"I know, like sometimes parents are only six months older than their puppies."

The puppy nuzzled Cricket. Cricket wanted a dog. Dog ears were so soft.

"Remember when Cadbury got mud prints on your mother's coat?"

"Yes. I think that might be why I'm allowed to go

to the park alone now. I will love Cadbury forever. What are you doing this summer?" Cricket asked.

"You're looking at it," Veronica said. "You know my family never goes anywhere. Except to the farmers' market."

Maybe Veronica could come out to the Hamptons. They could look for rocks on the beach and make stuff up. There's nothing like an old friend, a real friend.

Cricket was about to invite Veronica. But her parents always wanted her to hang out with the kids in the Hamptons, the kids whose families had money to give to their fund. Plus they were so scared about not getting their deposit back, they didn't want any extra people in the house.

If Cricket invited Veronica, Bunny'd force her to make up some reason why she had to disinvite her.

It's one thing to make things up because you want to. But it's another thing to make things up because your parents force you to.

10
BRAIN SURGERY

Bunny Cohen didn't understand that just because a person didn't want to rewrite a memoir, or do a math packet, or read and log a bunch of kids-dying-of-cancer books, that person was not necessarily lazy. Cricket was not lazy. She was not a dawdler, a procrastinator, or a time waster. Cricket was anything but a time waster. In fact, if Cricket must be labeled, she was an overachiever. If only Bunny knew the truth. How many other eleven-year-olds on summer vacation were about to perform brain surgery on their turtles, for heaven's sake?

The turtle was prepped, and Cricket had arranged all the other stuffed animals on her dresser so they had a good view of the operating theater. This was a teaching hospital, after all. How could the residents learn if they couldn't see? Cricket's schnauzer assistant arranged a pair of nail scissors, tweezers, a glass slide from the microscope kit she'd gotten for her birthday, and a needle and thread on her nightstand.

Garbed in purple latex-free exam gloves and a surgical mask the nice hygienist had given her on her last visit to the dentist, Cricket was ready to begin.

"O'Malley," Cricket said to the schnauzer, "I'm making the first incision. Scissors." Gently, but with the confidence required of a surgeon, Cricket cut. Below the surface of the fabric lay a tangle of white, swirled innards.

"Can everyone see?" she asked the residents when she'd gotten the turtle's head open. "This stringy, cotton-like matter is what we must send to the lab. Tweezers."

Working carefully with the delicate silver tool, Cricket extracted some brain matter from beneath the flap opened by the incision. She arranged some brain tissue on the glass slide. Using an eyedropper, she placed biopsy fluid on the white fluff. Instantly the fluff collapsed and Cricket covered the slide with another piece of glass.

"Who will run this to the lab for further inquiry?" she asked.

All the animals volunteered. They all wanted to be on Dr. Cohen's good side. It was touching.

"Who are you talking to?" Bunny asked from the other side of the door. "Are you writing your memoir?"

Bunny was impossible and relentless. Not to mention so inappropriate. Dr. Cohen looked out at her students and her patient. She was very embarrassed. Did Bunny actually think this assignment from Mr. Ludgate was just going to fly out of her daughter's mind? It wasn't. Cricket wished it would, but she was very much aware of the pressing matter of her memoir. But summer homework was no reason to stop performing cutting-edge surgery. She had responsibilities to her patients and to the medical community.

And yet Bunny wasn't leaving. Perhaps the residents could finish the stitching. They had to learn sometime.

"Fannigan, you lead the team from here. I want nearly invisible stitches, like these, see?"

"Cricket, what on earth are you doing?" Bunny said through the closed door. Then Bunny entered the OR. Without clearance or scrubs or even a mask. Outrageous.

"I'm in the middle of surgery," Cricket warned, trying to maintain her professionalism.

"Darling, please stop playing and write that memoir. Please just get it over with. Oh! Good news. I got the supply list for surfing camp!"

That Bunny thought this was good news was depressing.

"You don't seem very happy. Honestly, Cricket, it is a very first-world problem to be less than thrilled about learning how to surf. I really wish you'd write that memoir. Everyone is counting on you," Bunny said, and left the room.

The best revenge would be to get it out of the way. Better yet, Cricket thought, she'd let Bunny bug her nonstop, not telling her that the memoir was finished.

Cricket took off her scrubs and got out her notebook. Maybe she'd write about how annoying her mother was. Actually, she'd love to write about her work with stuffed-animal brains, but it was made up and that didn't count. *You don't need to pretend to be someone you're not,* Mr. Ludgate had said. But if she was good enough she wouldn't have to redo this assignment. She started to pace. If only everyone weren't so obsessed with memoirs being honest. It would be fun to write about visiting Dodo in California. She and Dodo always invented stories about why a young girl was traveling alone across the country.

One story was that her parents were famous actors and she got sick to death of being away on location, on safari. Another story (Dodo's idea) was about a national spelling bee championship. Even though the Africa story was more far-fetched, the plane crew bought it. Not the spelling bee story, though. On that flight the attendants treated Cricket like a liar. Until Dodo showed up at the gate with a huge sign that said CONGRATULATIONS FEVER LIGHTNING SPELLING BEE CHAMPIONS. One of the flight attendants almost choked when she saw Dodo and the sign. But of course those stories were off-limits for the memoir. The truth was so complicated.

The view from her desk was dark and gloomy because that was what life in an air shaft was like. "Life in an Air Shaft: The Cricket Cohen Story." Why was titling memoirs so much more fun than writing them? Good question. And possibly a good title for something one day.

She peered through the grimy window, hoping to catch a glimpse of something in motion. Something happening. There were people who were lucky like that. They looked at the right time. Just as a shooting star was falling, or a murder was taking place, or someone was vacuuming in the window across the air shaft. Timing was everything. Cricket's timing was awful.

Yesterday an air conditioner had fallen out of a midtown office building window. It landed on the busy sidewalk without hitting anyone. A woman in a taxi captured the whole thing on her cell phone. It was a fluke, but she and her footage had been all over the news. That kind of stuff never happened to Cricket.

Everything stank. The idea of surfing camp was crazy. And going with Lana Dean would be horrible. She'd have to figure out a way to get out of it. What if she wrote her memoir about the way her parents didn't let their daughter make her own friends? They would deny that, of course. But why else would Bunny have signed Cricket up for surfing camp with Lana Dean this summer? Lana Dean's aunt was a Rockefeller or something, that's why. Bunny hoped to make the most of Lana's parents' guilt about transferring Lana to private school next year by proposing a huge donation to the fund.

Cricket stopped pacing and decided to tell her mother that she could take surfing camp and shove it. Or maybe a better tactic would be to tell her parents to save their money since they were so worried about being broke all the time.

She padded down the thickly carpeted hall, overhearing parts of her parents' argument spilling out from the kitchen.

"Your mother missed the appointment," Richard said. "She should pay for it. We bought her the apartment, for goodness' sake. We have to buy her a dentistry practice, too?"

Since they'd quit their previous jobs and started the Enrichment for the Public Fund, living on the edge of financial ruin was their favorite topic. The reward of changing a rigged system was supposed to be worth being broke. But they hated being broke.

"She pays, we pay. What's the difference?" Bunny said. "The point is, I bought her her own calendar. It's in her apartment. I go over it with her every Monday when we review the week. It is like having another child. If I don't get that tooth fixed she's going to look like a homeless person who crashed the gala."

Bunny fanned herself with a napkin. Cricket had heard enough.

"Good afternoon and salutations," she said, announcing her existence. "No more arguing, please."

"Oh, darling, we're talking about Dodo. No one is arguing." Bunny put her arms around her daughter. "Go write your memoir."

"I am!" Cricket said. She didn't leave the kitchen, though.

They weren't owning up to fighting, so she wasn't owning up to a blank page.

11
THE WORLD'S YOUNGEST PROFESSOR OF GREEK

The first day of Cricket's summer, Bunny asked Cricket to set the table for dinner. Cricket hadn't finished breakfast yet. She hadn't even started breakfast yet.

That, in a nutshell, was what living with Bunny was like. Some people referred to Bunny as a force of nature. But Cricket found nothing natural about accomplishing what Bunny accomplished in a day. What had her mother just crossed off her to-do list? A power walk with the mayor? Finishing a bunch of things that didn't need to be done until later?

Cricket was in the middle of teaching her Greek 101 class, but she left her students and went to the dining area. She got out the place mats and the napkins and put them on the table. She was arranging the napkins when she remembered that Bunny liked the beige place mats with the off-white napkins. She'd have to switch one of them. Since the napkins were less work to switch, she took them off. She went to the kitchen and got the glasses Bunny liked best. After setting the glasses on the table she went and got the plates. Then she remembered that she'd left her stuffed animals taking their Greek final. She ran back to the classroom and collected the tests. If any of them had cheated, they hadn't benefitted. It was doubtful anyone had even passed the test.

"If you're the geologists you say you are," Cricket said, "you can't help picking up a little Greek; it's everywhere. *Geo* is the Greek word for *earth*, after all."

Total silence. Teaching stuffed animals anything was very frustrating. A lot of the time they literally just sat there.

"*Geo*-logy, the study of the earth. Come on. *Meta?* Who knows what *meta* means?" she asked. "You guys, this is basic."

There was a knock on the door from Bunny.

"Did you set the table?" she asked.

"Yes," Cricket said.

"Are you writing that memoir?"

"Yes," Cricket said, looking under the manatee for a notebook and a pen.

"Cricket, you can't break your word. You gave Mr. Ludgate your word. Did you set the table?"

"Yes!"

"Don't drag it out. Come in the kitchen, I want to show you something."

"Brandon, you're in charge. I have to speak to Principal Bunny. Please behave. Work in pairs with your flash cards."

Cricket didn't want to go to the kitchen. She hadn't wanted to set the table either. But she obeyed both requests. No one thought she did what she was told, but she was actually very obedient.

Halfway down the hall she heard her mother complaining. "If I don't get Vivian's picture in the *New York Times* looking fabulous at the gala, well, that is the last donation we will ever get from her."

"Bunny, you will. And if you don't, you'll call that photographer from *Avenue* magazine and get them to do a feature on her. She owes you a favor, right?"

"Richard, you are so brilliant. I love you. Cricket! Guess what I just did?" Bunny asked, grinning ear to ear. "I will tell you. I just got three evil corporations to contribute matching funds! We are going to put the *public* back in *public education* after all. Your mother is hot stuff."

Bunny did a hot-stuff dance around the kitchen table that made Cricket very uncomfortable. Sections of the newspaper were strewn about and Cricket looked under them. She hoped to find food.

"Your mother convinced these CEOs that if they weren't going to stop polluting New York's drinking water, they could at least give us money," Richard said. "I was sitting in my kitchen, minding my own business, while your mother made the playing field a little bit more level. She made the world a little bit better."

"Cool," Cricket said. "Wait, I don't get it. They still pollute the drinking water?"

"Yes! But honey, now they pollute the water and give kids a chance. Before today, all they did was pollute."

Bunny's phone rang and she seemed relieved by the distraction. "Carolyn Petty," she whispered. Bunny always told everyone in the room who was on her caller

ID. "Carolyn! How are you? How is Dick? How is Geneva?"

Cricket decided to pour herself a bowl of cereal while her mother's fund-raising alter ego reached into Carolyn Petty's pocket and took all the money out without Carolyn Petty even knowing.

"Oh, Carolyn, this is just, well, just tremendous. We are very grateful." Bunny looked over at Richard and Cricket and gave them the thumbs-up. "Yes! So much pressure, we're all going to crack up, I know! I don't have any idea what I'm wearing yet either." Bunny rolled her eyes and pretended to hang herself. "It is such a struggle, I know! Thank you so much, Carolyn. You, too." Bunny hung up and took a gigantic breath of air.

"Do you have news?" Richard asked.

"Fifty thousand dollars! Which equals a hundred thousand now, thanks to the matching funds of the polluters." Bunny did another hot-stuff dance. Cricket wanted to crawl inside her cereal bowl.

"Mom, you hate Carolyn Petty," Cricket said.

"Please don't speak with your mouth full. *Hate* is a pretty strong word, young lady. I don't hate anyone."

Hate might be a strong word, but it was the right

word. "Okay, you really really really don't like Carolyn Petty," Cricket said.

"That's right. I really don't like her. But I do really like the things she and Dick support."

Bunny and Richard shot each other a look.

"Cricket," her father said, "your mother and I are philanthropists. Furthermore, the Pettys, the Deans, the Greenburgs, for example, they all have too much money. Giving money to our fund is a tax write-off. It's good for them and it's good for us. We're all helping each other."

"So no one actually gives you money because they want to put the *public* back in *public education*? They just want to look a little bit less awful?"

Richard and Bunny looked at each other again.

"First of all, I love it when you say 'put the *public* back in *public education*,'" her mother said. "Second of all, I don't think you're ready to understand the nuances of fund-raising. Maybe when you're older." Bunny kissed Cricket and took her coffee down the hall to the converted linen closet that was her office.

Cricket wasn't in the mood to let anyone off the hook. "You guys either like the Pettys or you don't."

"Cricket, come on. It's not that simple," Richard said.

"Really? 'Cricket, either you went to Iceland or you didn't.'"

Her father wouldn't take the bait. "Did Mom tell you the theme for this year's gala?" he asked.

"No. But I bet you're going to."

"Sass, Cricket. Tone it down. The theme of this summer's gala is the circus. I think we have a really good chance of raising about thirty million with those matching funds."

It would be so satisfying if her parents rolled around in piles of money after a fund-raiser. If they raked it in like autumn leaves. But they didn't. They got checks in the mail and collected donations online.

"I thought the goal was five million."

"It was," her father said. "But with matching funds, we can go a lot higher. We could really do great things with that kind of money. Cricket, do you know why we do this?"

"To put the *public* back in *public education*?"

"Well, yes. But how do we know the public school system needs this? From you. From you going to public school. We do this for you."

"Well, thanks. I guess." But Cricket didn't see what their fund had to do with her.

"One day you'll be proud of what we do," Richard said. "I hope."

"One day you'll be proud of me, too," Cricket said. "I hope."

But she was doubtful.

12

ABBY QUITS

The doorbell rang. Cricket looked through the peephole and saw part of Abby's arm. Unlocking the rigmarole of bolts and chains and opening the door revealed the rest of Abby. Dodo, too. Dodo had an especially sweet look on her face. She winked at Cricket.

"After you, Mrs. Fabricant," Abby said.

"I told you to call me Dodo, nobody calls me Mrs. Anything," Dodo said.

"Maybe when you behave we can try that," Abby

said. Abby loomed over Dodo. They faced each other like cowboys in a standoff at high noon.

"After you, Mrs. Fabricant," Abby said again. Dodo made the face Cricket made when she got in trouble with a teacher who had no sense of humor. It was a look of proud indifference. She may have gotten in trouble, but it didn't count because it was with the uncool, no-sense-of-humor teacher.

"Mrs. Cohen?" Abby called.

"She's in her office," Richard said. "What's the problem?"

"I am needed but not wanted; that is something I am used to. But I have never been treated with so little respect. In my life. You saw my references. You saw what the man from the bank said. I told you how much of a gratuity that family left me. They were very pleased with me. It says so right on my credentials."

Dodo and Cricket hovered in the doorway.

"Dodo, what did you do?" Cricket whispered.

"I gave her the slip," Dodo said.

"Where?"

"In the park," Dodo said, obviously proud of herself. "I gave her the slip."

Cricket high-fived her grandmother.

"Abby, don't quit. Let's try and figure this out."

"I'm needed but not wanted," Abby said.

"You are needed and we do want you," Richard said. Then he yelled for Bunny.

"I don't want her," Dodo said as her daughter stepped into the kitchen. "Bunny, you hired her. Let her follow you around." Bunny moved closer to Richard.

Cricket made herself comfortable. This was going to be better than anything else that would happen today, probably.

"Richard," Dodo said, "may I please have a cup of your coffee? Abby refuses to make me a cup of coffee worth drinking."

Cricket felt like she had front-row seats at Wimbledon. Richard gave Bunny a helpless look and went to the machine and poured his mother-in-law the last cup of coffee.

"Abby, what happened?" Bunny asked, then glanced at Dodo sternly. "Mother," she instructed, "sit down. We have got to work this out. Sit, Mother."

Dodo did what her daughter told her to do. Bunny had that effect on people. Abby gave Cricket a look that made Cricket nervous. She found herself moving closer to her father. To the place Dodo had occupied moments before.

"Mrs. Cohen," Abby began, "I have been here for three weeks."

"You have. Please, call me Bunny," Bunny said.

Cricket would never understand how anyone, particularly her mother, the commander in chief and CEO of everyone's life, could prefer being called Bunny. Was that supposed to take the sting out of her orders? The word *Bunny* coming out of giant Abby's mouth would be hilarious.

"I told Mrs. Fabricant, and I will tell you, that as soon as I am treated with a little bit of respect I will call you whatever you like. But not until then. No."

"Richard, I think I need another cup of coffee, too," Bunny said, and Richard hopped to it. Cricket followed him to the sink. She measured out the coffee for him and got down mugs from the cabinet.

"Monday," Abby continued, "your daughter helped your mother try and fool me. Fool me once, shame on you; fool me twice, shame on me."

Cricket knew she was turning beet red. She also knew not to look at Dodo. If she did, she'd laugh, and then Abby might pick them both up and hurl them through the kitchen window.

She could feel her parents judging. They were never

going to understand how mean Abby could be. What had equaled fun and justice a few days ago wasn't going to be easy to explain today.

Abby turned on Cricket. "Look at her, she knows what she did was wrong," she said.

Dodo looked at Cricket, her co-conspirator.

Richard turned the coffeepot on.

"What exactly did my daughter do?" Bunny asked.

What was Abby going to say? Not the truth about herself, which was that she was patronizing to Dodo. She would never say that all she did was talk about herself and the famous families she'd worked for and that she never wanted to know anything about Dodo. She'd never say that all she did was watch TV and bark orders at Dodo. She'd never admit that she was the kind of babysitter who acts very nice in front of the parents and then is impatient and disinterested with the child when the parents are gone. Except that Dodo wasn't a child. She was a grown woman.

"The next day your daughter asked to take her grandmother for a walk. I was not invited. Then she refused to answer my calls. I told her I was off duty at five, I had to visit my grandson, and I told them to be back before then. I cannot leave the apartment until I have fed Mrs. Fabricant. And your daughter would not answer the phone and she did not come back until six and I was late to visit my grandson. I like to see him before he goes to bed. For all I know, she was probably involved in this morning's antics as well."

"I'm so sorry, Abby," Bunny said. "That is awful. Will you be able to see your grandson tonight?"

"Yes, he lives with me."

Typical Abby: exaggerate a story to suit her own needs.

"Cricket, why didn't you answer your phone? That's why you have it, so that you can be reached."

"My phone was basically dead, so I texted her," Cricket said, "and told her I had Dodo and that we'd be home later. I told her to leave, because Dodo was having dinner with us; it was on the calendar that we were having dinner together. You want to look at my phone?"

"Abby, did she?"

"Yes, she did, but I texted her back and I said that I couldn't leave till I had given Mrs. Fabricant her dinner. That is my job. To feed Mrs. Fabricant. My job is to cook for and feed Mrs. Fabricant. I am hired to do a job that no one wants me to do. In my business you are as good as your references. I have excellent references. You know that. You read them. That is why you hired me. No one in my care ever had bedsores. No one in my care ever had dry skin. Mr. Rothstein adored my cooking; he wanted to bottle my corn chowder. You know that the banker took very good care of me. I told you he died three weeks after I was hired but the family loved me so much they left me a very nice gratuity. They took very good care of me. Very good care of me. That is how I know I am very good at my job. My references and my gratuities when the job ends."

There was an awkward silence, which Dodo broke. "Well, I don't know about anybody else, but I don't think your corn soup is so hot and I'm tired of hearing about your references and gratuities. Abby, maybe you would be happier working with someone closer to their funeral so you could get your gratuity faster. But I am not dead yet."

Dodo then got up from the table and walked out of the apartment. But first she gave everyone the finger.

"I am a churchgoing woman," Abby said. "This is the rudest family I've ever met. I quit. You have my address; I will expect to see my final paycheck in the mail. Goodbye."

Cricket went after Dodo. What a morning. What a summer this was shaping up to be!

Dodo was halfway down the hall to her apartment when Cricket caught up.

"Hi, Poopsie! Did she quit?"

"She did," Cricket said. "Congratulations."

They walked into the apartment, which had the unique smell of Dodo. Lemons, cedar, and lavender.

"I don't want an Abby, I want a life. I told your mother that."

"Well, my mother doesn't always listen to what other people want," Cricket said. She thought Dodo should know that. She was older than Cricket was.

"Come, sit. What's the hot gossip?"

"I have to rewrite my memoir for school," Cricket said.

"Why?"

"Because I made up a story that I wished was true, but wasn't."

"Well, that doesn't seem like a crime. Remember when we used to make up stories? We haven't done that in a while. We should do it some more."

13

CRICKET OFFERS TO HELP

When Cricket returned to her apartment she felt like they should all celebrate. But Bunny was a wreck. A shadow of her usual triumphant and accomplished self.

"Bun, life is full of things you can't be prepared for," Richard said to his wife.

"I'm not prepared for life, then. Between my mother and the gala and finding a house, I feel like I'm going to have a stroke. I feel like I'm being buried alive. Every summer I forget how hard pulling this off is. It's like childbirth. I just block it right out of my mind. No one in their right mind would do what I do," she said, walking to her calendar. All the little squares with tasks and times and lists seemed so soothing to her. "Oh my gosh! Richard, we're supposed to spend the next two days with the Realtor!"

"Bun, I know that. So?"

"Abby! Abby was going to spend tomorrow night with my mother. Abby was the golden ticket." Bunny traced over the writing on the calendar with her finger as though it could magically bring Abby back.

"I can stay with Dodo," Cricket said.

Bunny and Richard looked at each other.

"Here's the thing, Cricket," Bunny said, "now that Abby's quit, I need help with Dodo."

"I just offered to help. You never notice!" Cricket said. "I like being with Dodo. You guys are the ones who act like she's a big problem."

"It's different for your mom. Dodo is her mother," Richard said, pouring another cup of coffee.

As mothers went, Cricket thought Bunny was way more problematic than Dodo.

"Let's think this through, Richard. Maybe Cricket could stay with my mother. What if we played it by ear? Generally that kind of idea is like nails on a chalkboard, but what if we leave tomorrow, and dare I say, see how it goes?" Bunny pretended to hyperventilate. Sometimes she made fun of how controlling she was. "If Cricket needs us to come home we will. And if not, we'll stay overnight like we planned."

"Why don't you call Dodo and see how she feels about it," Richard suggested.

Bunny went to the phone.

"We'll be fine," Cricket said. "We'll just watch old movies and play gin. And order out for pizza. We had sleepovers for weeks at a time in California."

"Just write your darn essay and get it over with. Please. Do the right things. Be responsible about this. Okay?" her father asked. "And for the love of Pete, keep your phone charged. That's why you have it. So we can reach you."

Bunny came over and gave Cricket a hug. Finally Cricket was being appreciated for pitching in. Bunny looked over her daughter's head to the dining area. Something was wrong over there. But Cricket wasn't sure what.

She went over the usual infractions but couldn't imagine the problem: her backpack was hung up, she'd made her bed this morning, she'd taken her shoes off by the front door . . .

"Cricket, I thought you said you set the table," Bunny said as she walked to the table.

"I did," Cricket said, joining her. Bunny was positioned at one end of the table.

"I'm confused," Bunny said.

"By what?" Cricket asked.

"Forks," Bunny said, "there are no forks. I don't mind that you didn't set the table, I mean I do mind, but what I mind more is you lying about setting the table."

"What's going on?" Richard asked, wandering in.

"Cricket told me she set the table. And she didn't," Bunny said.

"Oh, Cricket," Richard said. "Mom asked you a simple thing, to set the table."

"But I—" Cricket started to explain.

"Tables are either set or they aren't," Bunny said.

Humiliation gathered itself into a tight ball in Cricket's throat. She was about to cry. What was their problem? She had obviously begun setting the table. That was why the table had napkins, water glasses, and plates on it.

She marched into the kitchen, opened the cutlery drawer, and returned to the dining room with three forks. She put them on top of the napkins. She had a fantasy about stabbing and scratching the polished tabletop with their modern three-tined forks that were impossible to eat with but would make really good vandalizing instruments.

"Thank you, honey," her mother said. "I'll tell you what, why don't we have a race? I'll try and line up something worth ten thousand dollars for the auction by dinner, and you finish your memoir," Bunny said cheerfully. She went back to her closet, completely unaware that she'd hurt Cricket.

"She's on edge," Richard said, by way of defending his wife and recusing himself.

"She's always on edge," Cricket said.

"Well, that's true," he said, almost smiling, "but summer is always worse and this summer we really have to band together because now we don't have Abby. We have to pull our weight."

"I do!" Cricket said. She got groceries at Bilson's. She set the table. She walked Dodo back to her apartment all the time. And she was making it so they could go away overnight to the dumb Hamptons.

They never noticed when she did something good.

She should run away. She knew how. There were so many books that were practically how-to manuals on the subject. She went to her room and closed the door. Okay, slammed the door. Really hard. She pulled up her blanket and bunched her winter coat and a towel from the floor into the shape of a body under the covers. That was the first thing people running away from home did.

They sculpted a decoy body. In the morning when your bumbling and clueless parents finally came to wake you up, they discovered you were gone. You'd run away hours before. You were already across state lines.

When Claudia from *The Mixed-Up Files of Mrs. Basil E. Frankweiler* ran away, she used her instrument case as luggage. Too bad Cricket had quit the violin in second grade. She'd have to use a duffel bag. Although, how much stuff could you really fit in a violin case?

She was so tired of being subappreciated. *Sub* was Latin for *under*. She was so, so underappreciated. She grabbed jeans and shorts, socks and underwear. All went in her duffel bag. She never wore dresses; should she take one?

The next step of running away was tying a bunch of sheets together and making a ladder to throw out the window. Cricket lived on the sixth floor. She'd probably need like twenty sheets to make it the whole way down. And when she landed, she was going to land in a Dumpster. Gross. If she lived in the suburbs she'd be climbing down from the second floor to land in grass. She cut the Dumpster-landing scene. She'd escape through the living room window. Much more visually appealing.

A crowd would gather. Traffic would be held up. Maybe reporters from the news would come. Nosy Pete the doorman would call her parents on the intercom to tell them their daughter was climbing out the window. They'd run out and wait for her to get to the ground, panic-stricken, terrified. Her mother would be gasping, clutching at her chest. Cricket would reach the ground, drop her bag, and run into her arms, ready for her mother to apologize.

If only Dodo still lived in California. Cricket would run away to there. It would be an epic cross-country adventure. When she arrived, Dodo would take care of her. They'd eat great food, Cricket would learn to play bridge, they'd drive in Dodo's bouncy Cadillac, swim in her pool. But Dodo lived down the hall now, so California was out. And Cricket had already told her parents she was sleeping there tomorrow night. The stuffed animals looked worried.

"I'm not going anywhere," she told them. "I'm spending the night with Dodo tomorrow. I can't run away."

They still looked worried.

14

FATEFUL FRIDAY

Friday morning, the second day of her summer vacation, Cricket woke up in her bed at home.

"I told you I wasn't going anywhere," she said to the schnauzer. And speaking of going, Bunny was running around getting her real estate listings ready and doing Lord knows what else before they left for the Hamptons house hunt at ten a.m. Cricket suspected she'd have to make her own breakfast, but the biopsy results were back, so there wasn't time for breakfast anyway. She went right to the lab and got to work.

Her suspicions were confirmed. Every biopsy showed

the presence of White Cloud Disease. That was the reason all the animals had forgotten the Greek they'd learned over the past year. Her heart sank. She'd been way too hard on them. She'd assumed they just weren't trying. But White Cloud Disease lowered the brain's resting temperature, inhibiting the synapses from firing properly. A thick, cold film formed over everything. It wasn't fatal, but your memory was affected. Cricket made her morning rounds, trying to be gentler and more complimentary than usual. Then she went to the kitchen.

Her father must have had a grueling morning shaving because he had lots of toilet paper scraps stuck to his face. He looked like a folk-art pillow from a craft show.

"Good morning, Cricket," he said.

Cricket could tell he was stressed-out.

"Good morning, honey," her mother said. Bunny looked perfect.

Richard put three slices of sprouted-seed bread in the toaster. He kept trying to lower the bread slices in the toaster but they kept popping back up. He was so agitated he nearly broke the thing.

"Dad, it's not plugged in, that's why the lever won't stay down," Cricket said. "You're really looking forward to renting a summer house, huh?"

He was going to have to write a large check today. A deposit for some cockamamy house he couldn't afford. The Cohens were going to go into massive debt so that Bunny could raise the money she needed for the programs she'd designed to help people with less privilege than she was born into. And he'd had to give up gluten in the process. Bunny had decided the family was going gluten-free. Her husband complained about it all the time.

Cricket plugged the toaster in for her father and pushed down the lever.

"Thank you. How is that paper going?" he asked. "Can I see what you've written?" He loaded up the blender with protein powder and flaxseed.

"No."

"Why?"

"Because I don't want to show you," Cricket said.

"Because you haven't written anything. Have you written anything?"

"Yes!"

"I don't believe you. At all," Richard said. He looked at Bunny. It was clear that neither of them believed her. He turned on the blender.

"Cricket, why haven't you started your memoir?" Bunny called over the sound of her smoothie being made. Sometimes Bunny could hear through walls, above jackhammers, from other cities. "Oh, Cricket. I don't know what to do about this. You'll have to make your own bed with Mr. Ludgate."

But Bunny couldn't leave it alone.

"All right," she said at the calendar, with a mechanical pencil in her grip and hope in her eyes, "today is Friday. It is due to Mr. Ludgate on Monday." Bunny looked up and made eye contact with her daughter. "So, if you begin writing today and don't procrastinate, you can have a draft by . . . What is this dinner on the fifth of July, Richard?" Bunny asked with concern.

Cricket handed her father the almond butter.

"The Lysanders. At the beach," her husband said. He was trying to butter his gluten-free sprouted toast without crumbling it. "Bunny, this is a fool's errand."

"What is?"

"Spreading anything on this crazy cracker of a piece of bread. It's like trying to butter crumbs."

"The Norwegians do it. But I don't remember anything about the Lysanders," Bunny said. "I don't like forgetting things. It makes me feel old. Is it hot in here?"

"No. But do we even have a house yet? Maybe we should spend the summer here?" Cricket asked. That was one way of avoiding surfing camp.

"Daddy and I are finding a house today, no matter what. And if not today, tomorrow," Bunny said, like a mind reader. "I wish you'd look at the calendar, Cricket. Your whole life would be so much easier. Everything everyone needs to know is right there. No one in this family pays any attention to the calendar. We're spending the day with the Realtor, it says so right here, and we aren't coming home until we have a house. You might have to move in with Dodo."

"I didn't remember about the Lysanders either," Richard said. "But Jim e-mailed me yesterday. So I wrote it down. If you're losing your mind, I am, too."

"In red? Oh, Richard."

"Please don't be so controlling—at least I'm making an effort to use the calendar. Don't get mad at me for using the wrong color on it."

"I'm not being controlling," Bunny said carefully, tracing Richard's red-pen letters over with a blue marker. "I'm being neat. And organized. A system is only a system if it is followed." She turned and faced her daughter. "All right, young lady, as I was saying, finish the draft Saturday afternoon and then you can polish it up and be all done by Monday."

"Are you serious?" Cricket said.

"Are you? That's the due date, Cricket. This one is

going to be so much easier since you don't have to make anything up."

"It's harder if I can't make anything up," Cricket said. Her mother would never understand. Most days she ran through the apartment waving her checklists around like a child with a good report from her teachers.

Bunny wrote the due date for her daughter's memoir on the calendar.

"Mom!" Cricket said.

"Cricket, you don't have a choice. You gave Mr. Ludgate your word," Richard said. He made an offering of the smoothie he had just blended. "Bunny, she's got to get that thing finished."

Cricket didn't like the smoothies her parents drank and she didn't like the way they were nagging her either. She opened the fridge and was greeted by rows of colored organic fruit and vegetable juices. Bunny would be the perfect astronaut, content with neatly labeled packets of freeze-dried food that required no cooking.

"Cricket, your mother and I are leaving in twenty minutes. Maybe you'll accomplish more without us hounding you. Bunny, where is the jam I like?"

"Richard, I don't want to leave her alone."

"Do you want her to write the memoir or not? She'll be fine. There's a doorman. We've left her alone before.

And when she's lonesome, she'll walk down the hall to your mother's."

. . . . . .

Cricket stayed out of her parents' way as they bickered and got in each other's way, even though they were only packing one small suitcase for their weekend trip. Finally goodbyes were said and the front door was closed and triple-locked behind them.

Her father was right. All she needed was to be left alone. She'd absolutely get the assignment written. She walked from one end of the apartment to the other, confused by her brain. It was usually large and expansive and on the verge of brilliance, but today it felt dark and small and empty. Maybe she had White Cloud Disease.

What was there to write about? The houses her parents rented every summer? The life she was required to live while her parents entertained people they didn't like in order to get money out of them to give to the Cause they cared about?

Maybe she could write about Veronica Morgan, the friend she had taken for granted?

She'd feel better after a cup of tea. An idea would

definitely come after she had a good, strong cup of tea. She filled the kettle and turned on the stove.

The wall phone next to the refrigerator rang.

"Cricket, it's Mom."

"Hi, Mom."

"I don't like this whole business of leaving you alone."

"I'm fine."

"Please keep your phone on and charged at all times. And take this receiver into your room. I don't want to worry. I love you. And please check in with Dodo every now and then."

"I will. I love you, too. Come back with a good house."

"We will. Be careful. Don't use the oven. Or the stove. Don't let Dodo use the oven. No roast chicken."

"Okay."

"Daddy wants to say something. I'm putting you on speaker."

"Okay." Cricket held on to the phone between her shoulder and her cheek so she could rummage in the freezer. She found some croissants from a fund-raiser breakfast a few months back.

"Cricket? It's Dad. We love you and trust you. Be careful. Keep your phone charged. It's not a phone if we can't call you."

"Okay, Dad. Don't spend too much money. It's not

money if we don't have it." She took the bag out and turned on the oven to preheat.

"That's my girl. Love you tons. Write that paper."

"I am!" Cricket said.

. . . . . .

She wasn't. She put her pastry in the oven and drank her tea in front of the television after making her bed. She then went back to the kitchen, threw out her tea bag, which she had left on the counter, put the milk back in the fridge, put the bag of croissants back in the freezer, and wiped off the honey she'd dripped on the counter. Then she turned off the oven and waited for her hot croissant to cool down. She'd successfully wasted twenty minutes. Procrastination be thy name. She was on a roll!

Her parents always said that life included doing things you don't want to do. *Do you know how many things I do because I have to?* her mom would say. *Welcome to the real world,* her dad would add.

Cricket didn't like the real world. That's why she'd gone to Iceland in her memoir. What if she could turn this around by pretending Mr. Ludgate wasn't making her write the essay? What if she herself just wanted to rewrite her memoir? (Why anyone would choose to re-write a perfectly good memoir was anyone's guess, but this was the game and she was playing.) She went back to her desk and started thinking of titles:

"Life in the Air Shaft: The Cricket Cohen Story."

"Subappreciated: The Cricket Cohen Story."

And then her favorite:

"Rocks for Brains: The Cricket Cohen Story."

She had a lot of titles. Three! If only she had a story.

15

THE YELLOW COUCH

At eleven o'clock her life was still too boring to write about. So she turned the oven back on, put in another croissant, made a cup of coffee the way Dodo had taught her, put the croissant on a pretty plate, got a napkin, filled a little ramekin with jam, and arranged it all on a tray.

Dodo adored nice food and a good presentation. That was one of the reasons none of the people hired to look after her worked out. Every applicant bragged about being an excellent chef. But vinaigrette was the measure of a person for Dodo, and Abby's wasn't even homemade.

It was from a bottle. If a person failed at vinaigrette, Dodo never forgave.

"Room service," Cricket said, knocking on Dodo's door. When Dodo first moved down the hall they had played this game every day. Dodo loved hotels.

"How wonderful!" Dodo said, opening the door. "Set it over there, would you?"

"Dodo, can I fix your blouse?"

"What's the matter with it?"

"The buttons aren't lining up," Cricket said.

"Oh! By all means. When I was younger, my mother told me my favorite thing to say was *Byself.* I wanted to do everything by myself. What's the hot gossip?" Dodo said, and closed the door.

Cricket put the tray down on the kitchen counter so she could rebutton her grandmother's shirt.

"Mom and Dad left."

"They left us alone?" Dodo said, with a twinkle in her eye. She ate her croissant and drank her coffee. "Cricket, where did you learn to make such a good cup of coffee? It's so important. If you can make coffee, an omelet, and a vinaigrette, you're all set."

"What about a roast chicken? I thought that was on the list?"

"It is!"

Cricket noticed a couple of bags of groceries by the kitchen sink, so she started unpacking them.

"Oh! Thank you, Poopsie. I forgot about those."

"Where does the mustard go?" Cricket asked.

"In the pantry."

Bunny's pantry was one shelf neatly lined with protein bars. Dodo's pantry was a small closet filled with spices Cricket had never heard of, sumac and turmeric and juniper berries. She had oils made from avocados and grape seeds, vinegars from all around the world. Cricket put the jar of Dijon mustard on a shelf next to six other identical jars of Dijon.

There was a container of chicken salad and a quart of milk in the grocery bag. She wondered how long the bag had been sitting out because they were both warm. She threw them out, just in case.

"Who's here?" Dodo asked.

"Me," Cricket said.

"Did you just hear a car pull up in the driveway?"

"No, did you?" There weren't any driveways on West Sixty-Fourth Street.

"I thought so. Is someone here?" Dodo said, walking to the window and looking outside.

"Dodo, did you forget you were in New York?" Cricket asked.

"I think I did," Dodo said. "I'm nuts."

"No," Cricket said. "You lived in California for a long time. It must be confusing."

"It is. I'm confused. What was I doing?"

"I don't know. What were you doing?"

"Oh, I was in the bedroom, come."

Cricket wondered when and if the house in California would ever stop being the place she thought of when she thought of Dodo. The house in California with all the sunlight and the artwork and the two different living rooms. Of course Dodo went back there in her mind sometimes. This house, this New York apartment, was smaller and darker.

Dodo's bedroom was at the end of the hall. There was an open suitcase on the bed.

"You're packing?" Cricket asked.

"Yes! I was packing. I've got to get out of here for a little while. I don't have a ticket yet, but that doesn't matter. Planes leave all the time for somewhere. Come on. You come with me. Let's have an adventure together."

"I'd love to."

"Look, I've packed all these things." Dodo proudly showed Cricket the contents of her suitcase: five pairs of white pants.

"Well, Dodo, I like to bring some underpants when

I go on a trip." Cricket said. She tried to remember what else she'd actually packed yesterday before giving up on the idea of running away.

"So do I!" Dodo said. "So do I." She went to her dresser drawer and took out three pairs of underwear and put them in the bag. "Socks? For me feet? *Me feet, me feet, me feet.*" Dodo made up a little song.

"Great idea," Cricket said. "Maybe a bathing suit?"

"I don't swim anymore. But I'll watch you swim. Remember when you were swimming in my pool in California and you almost drowned? I saved you."

Cricket remembered. She had still been learning to swim and had worked her way to the deep end of the pool by accident. Before Cricket had had a chance to realize she was in danger, Dodo had jumped in the pool, fully clothed, including her silk scarf and her sunglasses. She'd pulled her seven-year-old granddaughter out of the water to safety. They'd never told Richard or Bunny because they thought they'd get in trouble.

"I do. You saved my life, Dodo, and now I will do anything for you."

"Oh! And I would do anything for you, sweetheart. I love you so much." Dodo wrapped her freckled, droopy arms around Cricket.

They were almost eye to eye. Cricket was getting

taller and Dodo was getting smaller. It was the strangest thing.

"I need a nice wrappy thing for the plane. A thing you put around. For the air-conditioning. You know?"

"A shawl?"

"A shawl! I have the most beautiful shawls. I don't want to leave without them." Dodo rummaged around on her bed. "I can't find the one that's my favorite. From Italy. From that very last trip with Dodie, before he died. But maybe if we look together."

"Okay. What color is it, Dodo?"

"There are several. But the one I have in mind is very fine cashmere. It's blue but it's also peach. Abby wore it all the time."

It was hard to imagine Abby wearing anything of Dodo's; the difference in their sizes was too much.

"I'm not mad about it," Dodo said. "It's a beautiful shawl. It looks wonderful on everyone. I knew she'd steal it when she left. Everybody needs something for the road."

Cricket sat on the bed watching her grandmother engage in what looked like a game a very small child would play: a sorting game. Dodo carefully moved everything from her suitcase, very methodically, piece by piece, into a large canvas tote bag. Then when she'd finished, she took each of the things out of the tote bag and put them back, one by one, into the suitcase again. It was like separating an egg by carefully pouring the contents back and forth from one eggshell to the other. Dodo seemed endlessly busy with this task.

"Let me tell you something," Dodo said, carefully laying a pair of white pants in the tote bag. "I have tried to do everything in my life with a certain amount of grace and integrity. But aging gracefully might not be possible. Oh, Cricket, my biggest mistake was thinking I would never be old."

"I'm sorry," Cricket said.

"All right, enough of this dreary conversation. Let's get out of here." Dodo left the half-empty suitcase on the bed and went back to the living room. Cricket followed. They made themselves comfortable on the yellow couch. The one thing Cricket had begged her mother to let Dodo keep when she moved across the country was the yellow couch. Cricket had written a haiku about that couch in second grade:

The way I feel on
The couch with my grandmother
Is bright bright yellow

16
ART AND SCIENCE

The coffee table was from California, too, covered with art books and dishes of candy, like in its former life. Dodo loved treats, which meant that nearly any cabinet or drawer of hers had something sweet stashed in it. Art and candy, and a bright yellow couch: that was Dodo Fabricant in a nutshell.

"Did you inherit my love of Matisse's cutouts?" Dodo asked.

"I don't know," Cricket said. There was a book about the cutouts open on the coffee table. Cricket moved it closer and looked through it.

"What was so exceptional about the cutouts was his preoccupation with negative space. No one had done that before. It was like preparing for death," Dodo said. "What I love about Matisse is that when he got old and was unable to move the way he used to, he just invented a new medium. The cutouts are a whole body of work, a whole style of expression that gives dignity and purpose to the time in life when most people quit and stop trying. Here, look at this one. This is one of my favorites."

Dodo showed Cricket a series of blue-and-white images. They were of women, or shapes like women, dancing in a circle. Cricket could see what Dodo meant. The white shapes in the picture were as prominent and as beautiful as the blue shapes were. Your eye focused on the background and the foreground equally. It was hard to tell which, if either, was supposed to register more in your brain.

"Everyone is so thrilled about the accomplishments of modern medicine. But not me." Dodo sighed. "My hero, Henri, cut through it, he got right at the substance. Aren't they wonderful? Have you seen them at the museum?"

This was the thing about Dodo: when you worried that maybe she didn't know what was going on and was very forgetful, she'd surprise you by having the most interesting conversation with you.

"Dodo, no offense, but when I go to a museum I usually go to the Museum of Natural History."

"I am not the least bit offended. Art and science are the most important conversations worth having. They should be taught together."

Cricket had no idea how Dodo was going to justify that remark. Science was understandable and provable. Art was something else entirely. In fact, the difference between art and science was at the root of all the great stories she had heard about her grandfather and her grandmother. Her grandfather had been a doctor and a scientist. Dodo was an artist and had become a collector.

"You doubt your old grandmother. But I'm right. Why do you love rocks so much? Pass me that candy."

Cricket passed her grandmother a dish of gummy bears.

"Because they're always changing and they have so many stories to tell and people just walk all over them without noticing."

"Stories about what?" Dodo asked, chewing on a red bear.

"The world, the way things were, I guess." Cricket

was used to Richard and Bunny. They ignored her love affair with rocks, hoping it would go away before turning into something more serious.

Cricket put her head on her grandmother's lap. Dodo's fingers were bent in odd ways because of her arthritis. When Dodo put her fingers through Cricket's hair it was like being stroked by a glamorous bird with talons.

"The reason you look at rocks is why I look to art," Dodo said. "Scientists and artists want the same thing, to make sense of the world. Religion wants that, too. But let's leave that one alone. Your grandfather was a doctor, you know. But he was really a poet. You are a scientific artist. That's wonderful."

"Talk about Dodie," Cricket said. Cricket had never known him. She wished she had. She knew that he had loved ketchup. That navy blue was his favorite color. That he always picked out the chocolate-covered almonds from the bridge mix and ate them himself without sharing. But she hadn't had any adventures with him.

"He would have thought you were a miracle," Dodo said.

"Why?"

"We weren't the best parents, Cricket. I couldn't wait to start over. You were a new beginning."

"I don't think my mother thinks I'm the best daughter."

"Oh, darling. I wonder if that's part of growing up. How tragic. I promise you, she loves you. She's in awe of you."

"But I'm not organized and I like to pretend."

"Opposites attract. If everyone were the same, where would we be? The most boring place imaginable." Dodo rubbed her arms with her hands. "I'm cold. Will you go get me a sweater?"

Cricket wandered down the hall to the bedroom. The walls were lined with old photographs of her grandparents, Bunny when she was younger, Cricket as a newborn morphing into the eleven-year-old she was now. She'd been looking at these photographs her whole life. Like the yellow couch, these pictures made Cricket feel safe.

Cricket ran her hands along the sweaters hanging in Dodo's closet. She wondered what had happened to all her other clothes. Were they donated to strangers? She used to have way more. Cricket picked out a soft blue cardigan and took it off the hanger. It would make Dodo's eyes bluer, like cutouts in a Matisse collage.

Cricket returned to the yellow couch and put the blue sweater around her grandmother's shoulders.

"Families are incredible inventions, Cricket," Dodo said. "Dodie and I made Bunny. And she and Richard made you. Now I get to sit here with a little piece of all of us."

17

A WALK IN THE PARK WITH DODO

Hey, Poopsie," Dodo said, clapping her hands together. "Enough sitting." She had the twinkle in her eye Cricket loved. "We're on our own. Let's go have an adventure."

"Oh, yes!" Cricket said. "Let's run away!"

Yesterday she'd abandoned the thought of running away. But now it seemed like a great idea all over again.

The bag she'd packed yesterday was still ready.

She ran down the hall to her apartment, changed out of her pajamas, and threw on a pair of shorts and a T-shirt. She brushed her teeth, brushed her hair, and put on sunblock to make her mother proud. But she was running away from Bunny, so who cared?

With her duffel bag slung over her shoulder and the door securely locked, she went back to Dodo's.

"Are you ready?" Cricket asked.

"Hello," Dodo said, smiling. Her expression was one Cricket had never seen before. Like Dodo was either deep in thought or lost between ideas. If her eyes hadn't been open, Cricket would have thought Dodo was dreaming.

"I'm ready for our adventure," Cricket said, hoping Dodo would return from wherever she was.

"Oh, yes! I was waiting for you," her grandmother said. She got up and put on her trench coat, her scarf, and her sunglasses. Cricket put down her duffel bag in the hallway and fetched Dodo's rolling suitcase from the bedroom. They locked the front door and went to wait for the elevator. The beauty of this day was that Bunny couldn't stop them. If Bunny were here, instead of being an hour away, stuck in the usual traffic on the Long Island Expressway, she would be putting an end to this escapade. Dragging her mother and her daughter over to the calendar. Showing them that no one was going on any adventure anywhere because it didn't say so on the calendar.

When they reached the lobby, Cricket saw that Nosy

Pete was not at his post. She heard him rummaging about in the package room next to the mailboxes. Sneaking out was no problem.

In just a few moments she and Dodo were standing a half block away, deciding where to go.

"I love the park," Dodo said.

"Me, too," Cricket said. "Wanna start there?" Most of Cricket's adventures began there.

"Absolutely," Dodo said. They entered the park where Cricket usually did, between Sixty-Fourth and Sixty-Fifth Streets. The small wheels of Dodo's suitcase occasionally got hung up on the uneven pavement. The noise of the wheels was like a musical introduction to their impending arrival.

The walking paths in Central Park were a series of loops—lovely, but not very direct. It was like the designers hadn't been interested in efficiency. When Cricket was in a hurry to reach a particular destination, she often went off the path. But Dodo, sensible walking shoes or not, was no spring chicken and the luggage would be more of a nuisance off the pavement. Today Cricket would stay on the paths. The weather was very pleasant and the park was quite populated.

Cricket soon felt encumbered by carrying her duffel

bag and pulling Dodo's bag. So she stopped at a bench to consolidate the luggage. The duffel fit inside Dodo's suitcase easily, and now she had one fewer thing to carry. "Aren't you clever?" her grandmother said once they set off again.

Columbus Circle was just a few blocks south on their right. Cricket disliked the traffic and the subway being so close by. She guided them straight ahead, deeper into the park.

"I just love the energy. Don't you?" Dodo said. She stopped at a hot dog cart and pulled her wallet out of her small handbag. She and Cricket shared a pretzel, and they watched the runners and bikers streaming by on West Drive, which was closed to cars. "So many different kinds of people. Fitness types, dog walkers with their yapping animals, mothers and the nannies, so many babies. So many birds. So many people using one place in so many ways. It's terrific."

Cricket went to the park, for the most part, to avoid people, but out of respect for Dodo she acknowledged all the people that Dodo was enchanted by. She felt like a tourist in her own city. If she was a tourist, maybe she'd just flown in from Istanbul. Or returned from a long, cold winter in the Canadian Rockies.

"Dodo, can I show you one of my favorite spots?"

"Sure."

Umpire Rock was a place Cricket mainly went to with other kids. She hoped Dodo would like it as much as she did. She was about to introduce two very good friends who'd never met. Dodo would definitely appreciate the crowd assembled on top. The sun worshippers in various states of undress, the people napping, the man sketching, and all the kids climbing, pretending the rock was somewhere else.

Cricket could see her favorite rock behind the baseball fields. But getting Dodo there took a long time because Dodo wanted to spy and listen to a man playing his guitar. Cricket handled the introductions when they finally got there.

"This is Umpire Rock. Umpire Rock, this is Dodo."

"Charmed, I'm sure," Dodo said.

"This rock has had quite a life. It lived through an ice age."

"I'm pretty old, but I've never lived through an ice age. Did you get this from a guidebook? Your grandfather always liked to read from the guidebook," Dodo said.

"I've read about it in geology books," Cricket said. "This rock is, like, four hundred and fifty million years old. It's been underground and then came back up. It's kind of famous."

She wanted to show her grandmother the different kinds of erosion on display. Since they couldn't climb up and look at the top, they'd have to examine the sides. She nestled the suitcase in a little nook in the side of the rock and led Dodo around to another part.

"Where are we going?" Dodo asked. She followed Cricket carefully and slowly on a wood chip–covered trail. The ground was uneven from roots and stones. For the first time Cricket could understand someone being afraid of another person falling.

"Here," Cricket said. She placed her grandmother's hand on the splintered façade of her favorite rock. "This is what I wanted to show you. The top of the rock, where all those people are sitting, is very smooth from glacial drag. But this part isn't."

"Glacial what?"

"Glacial drag. It takes thousands of years for ice sheets to melt. As they do, they travel, dragging tons of debris with them. The Wisconsin Ice Sheet reached New York City, right where we are standing, about twenty thousand years ago. The ice weighed tons and tons. Can you imagine how much pressure bearing down that was?

That's a lot of scraping and smoothing. But right here is a different kind of erosion. A more subtle kind."

What they were touching didn't feel very subtle. The jagged pieces were sharp, like the work of an ax or an ice pick that had hacked away at the side of the rock.

"Every day," Cricket continued, "especially during an ice age, water seeps into tiny little holes on the surface of a rock. The water expands when it freezes and contracts when it melts. After a few million years of pressure from constant stretching and shrinking, the rock starts cracking from the inside out, until pieces start falling off."

"Cricket, that is fascinating. It occurs to me that what you are describing is so true. No good comes from exerting too much pressure, or from dragging anyone anywhere. You've got to just leave people alone."

Cricket had been referring to erosion, but she had a feeling Dodo might be talking about Bunny. Same principle, either way.

She helped Dodo back along the dirt to the paved path and then she retrieved their suitcase.

Where to go next? This was her park, not Dodo's. She surveyed the surroundings. They had Heckscher Ballfields nearby. But she knew watching a ball game wouldn't be appealing to either of them. As a West Sider, Cricket spent less time on the east side of the park, so naturally that seemed like the best direction for adventure. They made their way along the path toward the drive, which looped across the bottom of the park and ran up the east side. Strangely, the drive seemed more dangerous with all the bikes and the Rollerbladers and the joggers instead of the cars that usually traveled across town. Cricket took Dodo's hand. They'd always held hands before crossing streets because Dodo was the grownup. Now it felt like Cricket was.

As they walked alongside the drive, the sound of calliope music coming from the carousel was undeniable. As far as Cricket was concerned, three dollars still bought one of the best things in New York City. Cricket didn't think she'd ever stop enjoying riding the carousel, but she never went if she was alone—it would be embarrassing. It wouldn't be embarrassing with Dodo, and it would give Cricket a rest from pulling the bag. The bag was getting cumbersome. They bought two tickets and climbed on deck. They were the oldest patrons. All the kids wanted horses, preferably the ones that went up and down, so Cricket and Dodo had their pick of either of the two carriages. They arranged themselves on a forward-facing seat of a carriage pulled by two black stallions. If only these horses and this carriage could take them the rest of the way.

"Are you okay?"

"What?" Dodo said.

"It's loud," Cricket said.

"What?" Dodo asked again. The minute they started spinning, Cricket was surprised by the speed of the ride. They were flying. Had she been scared on it as a child? Or just excited? She didn't remember spinning this fast.

She held on to Dodo, who smiled and seemed to be enjoying herself. Cricket had no idea if they'd been sitting in their carriage for five minutes or fifteen before the music wound down and the spinning got slower and slower. When they got off, Cricket asked the man at the ticket booth how long the ride was. Four and half minutes, he said.

They decided to stay and watch the next several groups of riders. It was just as fun—and dizzying—as riding the carousel themselves.

"What a wonderful day," Dodo said. "Just wonderful."

"I'm glad you're happy, Dodo."

"I am, I really am."

By now they were more than halfway across the park. Cricket was trying to decide if they should go north and look at something, such as the statues of the poets by the Mall. No doubt a destination, but Dodo probably wouldn't want to walk that far and they happened to be right near one of Cricket's other favorite geological wonders.

"Dodo, look."

"I'm looking. What am I looking at?" Cricket pointed to a little grassy hill just west of the carousel. There was a boulder resting right on top. It looked like a prop from a *Flintstones* episode. Around it were a few rods of twisted metal, like an afterthought, to prevent the boulder from sliding and flattening someone or something underneath it into a pancake.

"A glacial erratic," Cricket proudly announced.

"Very nice. It's like a sculpture garden. Who thought to import it?"

"Um, God? Glacial erratics got here before there were trucks and cars. The Wisconsin Ice Sheet pushed a bunch of boulders from the Palisades on the other side of the Hudson River to this area. That's why they're called erratics. From the Latin word *errare*, which means *to wander* and a couple of other things."

"What an adventure," Dodo said. "I'm glad we wandered into it."

"See how there's all that pink in there? It isn't the

same color as the bedrock. Or as Umpire Rock. That's a clue that it came from another place."

Cricket didn't understand why everyone in the world wasn't in awe of these giant, hard things like she was. Bedrock, for example, was so strong, buildings all around the city were literally anchored to it. And yet as solid as it was, it was a responsive being. With enough heat and pressure, any rock bent, folded, stretched, buckled. Rocks literally changed chemical composition. Rocks changed all the time. So in this way, rocks were very much alive.

Some people wore their hearts on their sleeves. So did rocks. Bands of colors, patches of crystals, and grooves, for example, all relayed the experiences and the stories of a rock's life. After learning so much about the Matisse cutouts, Cricket was happy to teach Dodo a thing or two about erosion.

"These large mineral crystals here? See? It means that this rock cooled underground—the ground was like a thermal blanket and the magma cooled very slowly. When magma cools very quickly, aboveground, you get tinier crystals."

"I wish your grandfather was here for this. He loved crystals. Have you ever seen a crystal under a

microphone? He'd look at anything under a microphone. He found the patterns endlessly fascinating."

"You mean a microscope?"

"Yes, of course, a microscope. What did I say?"

"Microphone."

"Oh, for goodness' sake. Does that ever happen to
you? My ideas spread out until the thoughts get so far
apart the letters fall away. I can't see what I'm thinking
about. I lose the words. I'm sorry."

"Don't be sorry. I'm sorry. That sounds annoying."

"It's frustrating. What was I saying?"

"Dodie, looking at things under a microscope."

"That's right. The cells and the patterns. It was like
art to him. Did I take you to see the cutouts exhibit?"

"You didn't," Cricket said. "But you've shown me
books."

"Do you love them as much as I do?"

"Yes, because they remind me of you."

"Well, that Matisse was really something. He got old
but he kept living. Everyone is so excited about how long
people stay alive, but I'm not so convinced."

Cricket was officially tired of the suitcase. They sat
on a bench for a minute.

"But didn't people use to die in their fifties? Dodie

did, right?" Cricket asked. She knew Bunny was fifty years old. Dodo was seventy-five.

"Yes," Dodo said. "But dying over a longer period of time isn't really the same as living longer, is it? Matisse, though, what a story. He reinvented himself at the age of seventy. He had an affair with one of his studio assistants, he created some of his best work. I couldn't even get Abby to make a decent cup of coffee or have an interesting conversation. Imagine if I had an affair . . . Oh, what's the point? Nobody likes old people. Not even me. Cricket," she said, "I don't want another one of those companions."

Poor Dodo, she looked like all the spunk had been squeezed out of her. They were separated by more than six decades, but Cricket and Dodo were very much in the same boat. Bunny was in charge of both of them and Bunny was relentless.

They were pretty close to the east side of the park now, but Dodo wasn't complaining. Maybe they could hit Sheep Meadow and look at even more erratics. Maybe it was time to get a hot dog and have a picnic. They went under Playmates Arch even though it led them farther from the meadow because the name Playmates Arch was so silly and it was fun to imagine an adult Victorian man creating such a place. They were now under another spot in the looping road with all the runners and cyclists. The arched space was lined with long, beautiful stripes of yellow and red brick.

When they got out of the tunnel, their eyes were drawn up the path to a shirtless man on roller skates. He looked like he was dancing through space. His whole body was enjoying a kind of kinetic bliss.

"Look at him go," Dodo said. "He's in this world and some other world. He's somewhere else."

Cricket couldn't take her eyes off him either. He was ecstatic, flying down the hill toward the tunnel. The skater was listening to music and gaining speed down the small hill. He was dancing and Cricket wasn't sure she'd witnessed such private joy in public before. He was having an out-of-body experience, an exultation.

Cricket was, too, until she realized that he was going to crash right into them. She placed herself in front of Dodo like a human shield. The man's eyes opened. His eyes met Cricket's. They shared a split second of panic, trying to figure out how he would slow down and how she would get out of the way. Without knowing what she was doing she moved the suitcase out in front of herself. She didn't mean to, but she tripped him with it. He went flying. So did the suitcase. It skittered across the path into a tree, coming open as it flew. Cricket waited to fall, but she and Dodo were still standing. They'd held each other up.

When the man got to his feet he was mortified. What a rude awakening from his private dance trance. "I'm so sorry," he said. His headphones were tangled around his neck.

"Me, too," Cricket said to him. "Are you okay? I didn't mean to do that. Dodo, are you okay? Should we sit down? Let me look at you."

"I'm so sorry," the man said again. "I wasn't paying attention." He tried to wipe the sweat off himself and make himself seem more presentable. "Can I get you some water? Can I do something? Are you okay? I'm really sorry. I'm going to get you some water."

"Dodo," Cricket asked, "are you all right?"

"I'm fine, sweetheart. Just a little stunned."

"Me, too. I think. But maybe we should sit down. Let's sit down for a minute." Cricket deposited her grandmother on a bench in the shade. She could have prevented what had happened by just moving to the left or the right. She'd seen it all about to happen. But she'd frozen and hidden behind the suitcase. She looked at Dodo's pants lying on the path, imagining they were her and Dodo sprawled out instead. They could have broken some bones. Gotten concussions.

"Here you go," the man said, returning with bottles of cold water and napkins from the Dairy shop up the path. "I feel awful. Please, is there anything I can do?"

"No," Dodo said. "You go off and enjoy yourself. It's a beautiful day."

"Are you sure?"

"Yes. We will take care of each other," Dodo said. "Right, Poopsie?"

The man looked at Cricket. She had nothing better to offer, so he skated away. But he was no longer a proud peacock. He was a shrunken pigeon. Cricket felt sort of guilty.

Cricket and Dodo sat on the bench near the Dairy. They drank some water and Cricket gathered Dodo's pants. She repacked the bag only to discover that the zipper wouldn't close anymore and one of the wheels was broken. Everything fit in her duffel since Dodo hadn't gotten around to packing much. The days of rolling a bag around were over. Cricket threw Dodo's suitcase in a garbage can.

She pulled her phone out of her pocket and checked to see what time it was. Her phone battery was draining fast. Her charger! Where was her charger? Was it on the grass? Had it fallen out of the bag? She must have left the house without it. Yes, she had. She'd run inside, dressed, and taken her bag and hadn't bothered with her charger. It was still sitting on her desk in her bedroom.

She and Dodo had survived a near-death experience but when her parents got ahold of her they were going to kill her. How could she run away without a phone charger? She was so dumb.

Quirky, mournful music played nearby. It was a saxophone, and the tune was so familiar. She definitely knew the song, but the name of it kept slipping right through her brain. It was driving her crazy.

Dodo met the news about her suitcase with her usual easygoing attitude.

"You win some, you lose some. I lost that bag."

They walked toward the saxophonist. He was standing right outside another pedestrian tunnel, and his case was open with a few dollars in it. Cricket didn't have any money with her or she'd have thrown it in. The theme song from *The Pink Panther*. That's what he was playing. The music echoed ever so slightly in the tunnel. She and Dodo walked through.

18

THE PIERRE

Home was getting farther and farther away. Cricket knew that much. She also knew that home was where she was supposed to be. Home had telephone chargers. Home had the memoir she hadn't written. Home was the responsible direction to go in. But Cricket didn't like the idea of going backward.

Cricket and Dodo continued forward. Past the children's zoo they came upon a crowd gathered in front of the Delacorte Clock.

"Look," Dodo said, "we must be right on time." Given the number of people, Cricket guessed the bronze animals would begin their turn around the tower any minute now. She loved the distinct personalities each of the animals had. The hippo was so large and yet so sprightly on his feet while playing the violin. The kangaroo and the baby kangaroo were very serious. The goat with the pipes was pretty intense, too. The bear was fat and frolicky, and his whole body appeared to shake along with his tambourine. And the penguin marching with a drum was incredibly adorable. They all seemed alive even before they started marching around on the hour and half hour every day of the week. Dodo was the first person who had showed Cricket this clock, on a visit from California. She hadn't told her that all the animals would start moving. It was like magic when they'd all begun marching. Cricket had never been able to settle on a favorite animal.

She and Dodo waited with all the others and watched as all the animals made their way around the tower. The show was over when the monkeys rang the bell. People clapped and the crowds started to irritate Cricket. There were even more people at the entrance to the main zoo. An entourage of tourists pushed past them to get on line for tickets and Cricket decided she didn't like the east side of the park anyway. It seemed more fake. The zoo, the café, all the portrait painters waiting by the gate to the zoo—these were not the things that Cricket liked about the park, and she doubted Olmsted and Vaux would have liked them either. Cricket veered toward the exit onto Fifth Avenue. Dodo gripped the handrail of the stairway that led out and Cricket was right behind. When they emerged onto Fifth Avenue, she felt like an astronaut who'd successfully landed on the moon. If she'd had a flag, she'd have planted it to mark her arrival.

They may as well have been on the moon, that's how much the Upper East Side felt like another planet to Cricket. The only thing connecting her neighborhood and this one was that the Upper East Side was filled with the people who wrote large checks to her parents' Upper West Side Enrichment for the Public Fund.

Cricket wondered how many people passing her on Fifth Avenue had either bought a table for this summer's gala or knew someone who had.

"Did I ever tell you that I lived there?" Dodo said. She and Cricket were standing on Sixty-Fourth Street and she pointed down a few blocks to the Pierre Hotel. "I had an apartment on the seventh floor. It belonged to a client. But she let me stay anytime I came on art-buying trips or when I visited you. What a hotel. Those were the days when you actually had a room key. My key, I remember, weighed about five pounds. Every morning the person at the desk would say, 'Good morning, Mrs. Fabricant. Did you sleep well?' Talk about service. I remember it vividly."

They crossed Fifth Avenue and Cricket caught Dodo as she almost lost her footing at the curb.

"I always have to tell your mother, 'If I fall, I fall.' She thinks she can protect me. Cricket, do not ever take me to the hospital if I fall. Just leave me. Do you promise? I don't ever want to go to the hospital."

"Leave you on the ground? What if you're bleeding?" Cricket asked. If Dodo were on the street bleeding she would never just walk away.

"I don't want to discuss it," Dodo said. "I don't want to go to the hospital. I want to go to the Pierre."

Dodo took the lead at that point and the next thing Cricket knew she was walking past a very attentive uniformed man standing on a circular version of the hotel's logo embedded in the sidewalk. He wore a black top hat and white gloves.

"Welcome to the Pierre," he said, and he opened the door for them.

They entered an unassuming vestibule with some steps up ahead. Cricket couldn't understand how this could be the reception area of a famous hotel. There was no lobby that Cricket could see. But Dodo kept going, leading the way to a flight of stairs. She seemed much more limber now, and more confident.

At the top of the stairs, another man with white gloves and a long black coat greeted them with such a big smile, Cricket thought he might actually be a long-lost dear friend. The floor was black-and-white marble, with an even larger version of the Pierre logo emblazoned in the center. Now *this* was a lobby! The floor was so shiny it must have been polished every three minutes. Cricket could practically see her reflection in it, and she felt underdressed in shorts. There was a long desk and flowers everywhere and the two men behind the desk wore uniforms to match the black-and-white floor.

"I'm Dodo Fabricant," Dodo said. "I'm checking in." Cricket joined Dodo at the desk, flabbergasted.

"How long will you be with us?" a desk clerk with a name tag spelling *Casper* said.

"I don't know. We've run away," Dodo said. She handed him a credit card from her purse.

"Well, you've run to the right place," Casper said.

Cricket was standing next to a round table covered

by multiple glass vases filled with coral tulips. All the colors around her were so elegant and so understated. It was as if the whole experience was supposed to be a secret. Even the way you had to almost already know the location of the lobby. If Dodo hadn't known where to go, Cricket wouldn't have found the place where they stood now.

After tying a bunch of sheets together and climbing out the window in her mind, the Pierre Hotel was, well, a better place to land. This was the way to run away. Not even Claudia Kincaid, who hid in the Met with her little brother, had had it this good. As usual, Dodo had just taken everything to a new level.

The desk clerk gave them a large key, with an even larger fob. Just like Dodo had said. Another man in a uniform and white gloves appeared and removed the duffel bag from Cricket's grasp. He led them to the elevator. Another man in a uniform and wearing white gloves took them up in the elevator. They were really on vacation now—they didn't even have to push elevator buttons.

"I do so adore a man in uniform," Dodo whispered. At that moment Cricket did, too.

"Is this your daughter?" the bellhop asked.

"You are adorable, by the way," Dodo said. "This is my granddaughter; I could never have this much fun with my daughter."

On the fifth floor, the bellhop led them out of the elevator. The carpeting was so thick Cricket couldn't hear the sound of her own feet. The walls were papered in the palest apricot color. All the colors were so soft and subtle it was as if the hotel decorator didn't want the guests to be shocked by anything. Even the air smelled subtly like flowers and something green. The man opened a room and gestured for Dodo and Cricket to enter. It was pale blue with a view of the park. It was stunning.

"May I put your baggage on the stand?" he asked.

"You may," Dodo said.

Dodo surveyed two queen-size beds with silk bedding. She opened the drawers, the closets. She assessed the view. Cricket wondered if she'd be able to see Umpire Rock.

"The room is lovely, thank you. But we will need more bathrobes."

Dodo gave the man five dollars.

"My pleasure," the bellhop said, and left.

The second the door closed, Cricket's phone rang. It

was as if Bunny knew her mother and her daughter were up to something.

Cricket looked at Dodo and said, "Bunny." She answered the phone and said, "Hello."

"We've arrived," Bunny said.

"Us, too," Cricket said.

"I beg your pardon?" Bunny said. "You've arrived where?"

"Just kidding," Cricket said, panicking. "How was the traffic?" Her parents loved talking about traffic.

"Oh, Cricket, it was murder. They have got to build more roadways out here. It was like being strapped to the back of a snail, at the end of the world, in a fire. How's your memoir?"

"Really good."

"Good! Honey, I'm so proud of you. So you'll have a draft by the time we get back?"

"For sure," Cricket said. She took a deep breath, wondering why she said half the things she said. To make other people happy? To make herself happy? To avoid conflict? To make things worse? Whatever she'd avoided by saying she was working on her memoir was going to be irrelevant when her mother found out she hadn't written a word. And when she found out the other fact, that Cricket had run away from home? This was some crazy adventure she'd gone on with Dodo. She would definitely have some explaining to do.

Her phone battery was at 30 percent. Maybe it would die and she'd never have to answer it again.

19
OLD MOVIES

Dodo took Cricket to the Rotunda for afternoon tea.

"I think we're the first to arrive," Dodo said. "I wonder where everyone is?"

The room was round and the walls were covered in murals. Dodo said there were portraits of celebrities mixed in with the figures of Greek goddesses and historical figures.

Cricket spotted a double staircase in the middle that she had to explore while Dodo waited for a staff member.

The stairway led to a large banquet room where

Cricket guessed weddings and big parties happened. There were stacks of gold chairs, piles of white table-cloths, crates of dishes and silverware waiting for someone to arrange them. The walls were covered by murals as well. Even though the lights were off, the grandeur was obvious. But there was something scary about an empty room that was meant to be filled with people. Cricket felt the presence of previous guests. Like the room was filled with centuries of ghosts. She wanted to get out of there.

Dodo had seated herself at a round table. "Have you ever had tea?" Dodo asked.

"Well, yeah," Cricket said.

"High tea?" Dodo asked. "I don't even like it. But it is very amusing to be served so many ridiculous finger sandwiches. Cucumber and watercress and egg salad. And fresh scones with jam and clotted cream." She looked at her watch. "Well, I am very surprised by the service here, I have to tell you. They used to be so attentive."

"Wait, cucumber sandwiches and scones? I guess I've never had that. I thought you meant a cup of tea."

"I remember it being so busy. So many people. Why is everything falling apart?"

"Maybe they're on a break," Cricket said. She and Dodo were still the only people there.

"This poor hotel. Two years after it was built the Depression hit it and the place went bankrupt. Jean Paul Getty bought it for a fraction of the original price and it was back in business. Then many years later there was a heist. It was all over the papers. Eleven million dollars' worth of jewelry was stolen. The burglars came in a black limousine. They took hostages. It was like out of a movie."

"Wow," Cricket said. It was hard to imagine criminals with guns and hostages being held in terror against the backdrop of such luxury.

"I wish they hadn't stolen the tea," Dodo said.

After waiting a few more minutes Dodo got fed up. They made their way back to the lobby and she complained about the lack of service to the gentleman behind the front desk.

"Ah, madam, we no longer serve high tea in the Rotunda. There was no demand for such a formal meal. I apologize."

"No demand for high tea?" Dodo said. "I don't understand."

"Well, tastes change. It is a sad but true thing. However, if you will go back to your room we'd be happy to bring it up to you. Or you are more than welcome to order tea in the lobby restaurant."

"That is much too noisy. We'll go upstairs. Thank you."

Cricket's head was still reeling from being in such a swanky hotel, whether or not they had had high tea. After their run-in with the skater in the park, Bunny would have taken them to a hospital. Or to a lawyer to prepare litigation against the roller skater and the park. Or she would have returned them safely to West Sixty-Fourth Street to lock them up away from danger.

But because she was with Dodo, they'd taken their near fall and dusted themselves off and were embarked on a bona fide glamorous adventure.

They never ordered tea, but they did order dinner at six-thirty. Cricket let the room-service waiter in. He arrived pushing a rectangular rolling cart covered with a white cloth. In three deft moves he transformed it into a round table, set with dinner. There was even a vase of flowers. All the plates were covered by silver domes to keep their food warm. Dodo signed the receipt and closed the door behind the parting waiter.

"When I was a girl," Dodo said, coming to the table, "I'd cut school and go to the movies. I didn't care what was playing. The minute the lights went out, my heart would start pounding. In those days each studio had a reputation. MGM movies were always glamorous and sophisticated. Warner Brothers movies were cynical, even if they were romantic. I remember one morning I sat down next to a man and we looked at each other and it was my father! We were both so scared of my mother finding out we thought we'd die. We promised not to tell on each other. She would have killed us."

Cricket sat down opposite her grandmother and carefully removed the big shield over her steak dinner.

"What movie was it?" Cricket asked. Her steak was slathered in green peppercorn sauce and there was a side of french fries as well. Dodo had ordered lobster thermidor. Also french fries.

"I don't remember. But it was a good one. They were all—well, every one of them was good. Bette Davis was my favorite."

They ate dinner as though doing so in a posh hotel room in your own city was perfectly normal. There was nothing normal about it, but it was 100 percent fantastic. Cricket had never had more fun in her life. And if she told people she had run away to a hotel with her grandmother and eaten dinner in their room, no one, not even Lana Dean, would believe her.

"I loved Bette Davis," Dodo said. "The studios didn't know what to do with her. She was too talented for her own looks. She was always offered boring roles. There was a picture called *Of Human Bondage* and she'd been offered the lead, but she belonged to another studio. She asked them to release her and they were thrilled to do it, they didn't think she was attractive enough. Have I shown you that movie?"

"No, I don't think so," Cricket said.

"She should have won an Academy Award for that role. It was a very complex part. And even after doing it to such acclaim, she was still offered boring roles. So she actually took out an advertisement asking for someone to cast her in something worthwhile. She really got under people's skin. Someone observed, after she died, that she would have been burned at the stake as a witch if she'd been born a few hundred years earlier. That's what they did to women no one liked back then. Can you imagine?"

That was a pretty horrifying thought. Cricket could absolutely imagine Lana Dean and Juliet Lysander and Heidi Keefe starting an uprising. A movement to get Cricket tried as a witch.

"What Bette Davis films have I shown you?"

"*All About Eve* and *The Man Who Came to Dinner*."

"A drama and a comedy, see. She had quite a range.

As a woman, Cricket, you have got to be independent. You have got to create your own life or you'll get type-cast."

"What does that mean?" Cricket asked.

"It means people only see you one way. An ingenue. A leading man. Or, in my case, impossible."

"Or, in my case, an unreliable maker-upper of stories."

"Cricket, you have an imagination. That is wonderful. It belongs to you. As long as you have that you are going to be just fine. But listen to me: people will try and re-create you in their own image. It will be a struggle. In the end, though, it will be hardest on them. People have got to stop trying to make people be people they aren't. Your mother wants me to have one of those home aides. I've lived alone for twenty-five years. It took me a long time to stop crying every night after your grandfather died, to pull myself together, and I'm not about to become dependent on someone I don't even have a real relationship with. I've had enough reinvention in my life."

As if Bunny were eavesdropping, the phone in Cricket's pocket vibrated.

"Hello?" Cricket said. She prayed that her phone would die and that it would not die. Bunny's calls were stressing her out.

"Cricket?" Bunny said, as if unsure that Cricket was the one answering the phone.

"'Tis I," Cricket said.

"Cricket, there's no answer at home. Where are you?"

Hmm. Cricket didn't want to say she was in a hotel eating room service. Yet she was trying to keep the lying to a minimum.

"With Dodo."

"Is she behaving?"

"Yes." Cricket looked over at Dodo and mouthed *Bunny*.

"All right, well, we didn't find a house today. But we're hopeful about one tomorrow. It's made entirely of glass. How's your memoir, are you finished?"

"I'm working on it right now."

"Good girl, Cricket. I love you."

"Bye, I love you, too."

She really needed to stop lying.

20
REINVENTION

Was that Bunny calling to check up on me?" Dodo laughed. "Did she ask if I was behaving myself?"

"Yes, of course," Cricket said. "But Dodo, what were you saying before, about reinvention?"

"What was I saying?"

"Reinvention and how a woman has to be independent."

"She does. You're so right, Cricket. When your grandfather was alive, he worked hard and discovered important things and I packed our bags. He was the scientist and I was the wife. I organized our trips to conferences. I made arrangements for things to do and see between and after these conferences. We traveled all the time. I loved it. We went all over the world. But there was a hierarchy. Dodie and his work were at the top. They came first."

Cricket had a tremendous gift for imagining things. But this old-fashioned version of her grandmother was hard to visualize. The Dodo she'd known her whole life believed that women must take care of themselves. She said a woman shouldn't need a man. It was all well and good to want a man, but that was no reason to depend on one. The Dodo she knew was always surprising people. People assumed that a woman named Dodo would be a ditz (even though the same people were more than happy to think that a man named Dodie was a genius), but she was a formidable businesswoman.

"When your grandfather died, I was in a sinkhole of grief. I was miserable. But I had to support myself. I had to work. My friend Cassandra was a painting teacher at CalArts. She told me about some young people with talent and I began collecting. They were complete unknowns, but there was something about the silence of these young people's pictures that really spoke to me. I couldn't concentrate on reading, but I found I could look at art. I could see myself in the stories art was telling. I chose two artists to take on. I became their champion. That's the thing about the world, you're a nobody until you're somebody. One of those artists, well, you know the story, he got very famous. He's still very famous. So overnight I became important."

Dodo got up from the table and walked around the room. Cricket decided to put on her luxurious bathrobe and wash her dirty shirt in the bathroom sink using some of the fancy hotel shampoo. She hadn't packed a clean shirt.

"I have a yen to watch a movie," Dodo said.

"Okay," Cricket said. After hanging up her dripping shirt on the shower rod, she got the clicker and turned on the TV. She was more interested in hearing about Dodo's life than in watching a movie, but Dodo always picked such good movies.

"So before the Dodo I know, you didn't work?" Cricket asked. She was still having trouble wrapping her brain around that idea.

"Nope," Dodo said. "I was very domestic. I took care of Bunny and I took care of Dodie and then I spent six years with him and his cancer. Dodie and I were such an old-fashioned kind of marriage, our names matched.

Dodie wasn't his real name. It was a nickname to match me. He thought it was very funny. Your mother thinks I was very selfish. Can you ask the TV to show us all the Bette Davis movies they have? I want to see Bette Davis."

Cricket started spelling B-E-T-T. She figured they were going to be staying up late. Maybe they'd even order more room service.

A list of about fifty titles appeared and Dodo chose *Now, Voyager*. They propped up all the pillows on one of the queen-size beds and got comfortable.

The movie took place on a ship, in Europe, in a mansion, and at a mental institution. Cricket loved being transported. Dodo sat quietly, her face frozen in a look of amazement. Cricket squirmed under the covers when the characters in the movie reconciled themselves, for no good reason, to life without love. She couldn't believe the movie ended with the two people who loved each other not spending their life together. They could have been together so easily. All the man had to do was leave his wife, whom he didn't love, to be with the woman he did love.

"Dodo! Why aren't they together?" Cricket demanded when the movie ended.

"Because love is an illusion."

"Dodo! Do you really believe that?"

"I don't know. I've been alone so long, what do I know?"

Cricket turned off the TV and the room was dark. "Tell me more about Dodie." She climbed off her grandmother's bed and into her own.

"Well, he was very funny. He was very smart. I loved him with everything I had and if he hadn't died, I don't know if we'd still be together. Who knows?"

"Oh my gosh," Cricket said. Her mother had almost come from a broken home. This was all new information. Cricket was fascinated. But what her grandmother was saying didn't make sense. Dodie was the love of her life. Why wouldn't they have stayed together forever?

"I've had two very good lives. The one where he and I were together and we made Bunny. And the life I made for myself after he died. At the end we had the most languid and romantic time, traveling and trying to fit as much love into the year we had left. It is hard to describe what life's like when you know someone is going to die soon. I don't think Bunny thought I did a very good job. Sometimes you try and hold it together but another person just needs to see you fall apart. I was proud of myself for not cracking into a million pieces. But maybe Bunny thought I didn't love her father because I didn't let her know I cried into my pillow every night. To be strong."

"Why?"

"I didn't want her to worry that she had to take care of me. I was her mother, not the other way around."

"So you pretended not to be upset so that she would be less upset, but you made her more upset?"

"Something like that."

"Just like a Bette Davis movie. Dodo, you should have told her you were sad."

"I suppose I should have. But sometimes you want something that isn't true to be true. I didn't want to be so devastated. I didn't want Bunny to be devastated. I didn't do the right thing. She was very angry with me. She felt cut out of her father's dying, while he and I traveled, and then she felt that I wouldn't grieve with her. But I couldn't. It was too much grief for me. We didn't speak for a long time. And then you were born. We came back into each other's lives because of you."

21

THE MIX-UP

C ricket!" Dodo screamed.

It was the middle of the night and Cricket forgot where she was. She felt around for her glasses and remembered she was in a hotel. She sat up in her bed and found Dodo in a corner of the room, frantically looking through the duffel on the wooden luggage rack. A little table lamp illuminated her. It looked like a scene from a play.

"Where are all my clothes? Where is my suitcase?" Dodo continued. "I packed for days, and someone has taken all my things. All my beautiful things. Call the front desk. I've been robbed."

Cricket tied her bathrobe. It was two a.m. They were in the Pierre. They'd run away. Dodo had barely packed because when the packing part happened they didn't have a plan. It was just pretend.

"Dodo? What do you remember? Because when I was with you, you only packed pants. White pants. And underwear. Then we talked about socks and you were very busy with your tote bag and your suitcase and I don't know if you put anything else in your bag. I wasn't really paying attention."

"Cricket, I know how to pack. I'm an inveterate traveler. This bag was packed by an imbecile. I'm telling you I was robbed. Things are missing." She picked up the phone. "Hello, this is Mrs. Fabricant, room 509. There's been some kind of terrible mix-up and either I've been given the wrong luggage or I've been robbed. Yes, thank you. I will wait right here." Dodo hung up the phone. "This is just terrible. I wanted to go out for lunch. I can't go out in these clothes. They're dirty and there's nothing for me to change into."

"Dodo, I can wash out what's dirty, or maybe they even have a laundry service."

"That's a good idea. And then I'll put it back on, then we'll go shopping because I want to go to the Matisse show. But first they've got to catch the person who did this to me, why do people, why?"

Why indeed? Maybe her father was right and Dodo was losing it. It was the middle of the night and Dodo was ready to go to a museum. And to lunch. There was a knock on the door and a woman in a dark suit was standing in the hall.

"Hello, I'm Ms. Michaels, hotel security. Is there a problem?"

"Come in, come in!" Dodo said. "Your suit is wonderful. Is that yours, or does the hotel provide it? It's very handsome."

The woman looked like she was trying to assess if Dodo was harmless or up to something. Cricket wished they could compare notes.

"Can I get you a drink? Cricket, offer this man a drink." Cricket looked at Ms. Michaels, hoping for some direction. Should one of them, for instance, explain that Ms. Michaels was a woman? Cricket didn't know where to begin.

"No. No, thank you," Ms. Michaels said. "What seems to be the trouble?"

"The trouble is that everything I care about is gone."

Cricket hadn't ever seen Dodo this upset before.

"Cricket? Is that your name?" Ms. Michaels asked.

"Yes," Cricket said.

"Would you mind getting your friend here a glass of water?"

"Sure. She's my grandmother." Cricket went to the minibar and poured a glass of water and gave it to Dodo. "Here, Dodo."

"Thank you, Cricket. Please tell this man how terrible it is. How awful it is. How tea is gone. How everything is ruined and how everything is missing."

"Well," Cricket said. And then she didn't know what else to say. "Dodo. I think you're a little bit confused. We just checked in today. You used to stay here all the time on buying trips. And when you used to come, they served tea in the Rotunda."

"That's right. They did. I used to come here all the time. And I stayed on the seventh floor. This is not a buying trip?"

"No. We're just here, you and me."

"I think I'm confused. What day is today?"

"It's Friday. Well, actually, it's Saturday morning now. We're at the Pierre."

"I love the Pierre."

"So do I," Cricket said. "I think we both got confused

· 159 ·

when we packed. Because I didn't even bring my tooth-brush."

"The hotel can send up a toothbrush. Will that be helpful?" Ms. Michaels said, smiling to herself.

"Two toothbrushes. The hotel will have to send up two toothbrushes. Thank you," Dodo said.

"Two toothbrushes and then are we out of the woods?" Ms. Michaels asked, clearly hoping the case of the missing luggage was closed.

"Yes, of course," Dodo said in a way that implied all the confusion was the security officer's fault. Cricket showed Ms. Michaels to the door.

"Are you all right? You're a little young to be in charge of your grandmother."

"She's not usually like this. She's probably tired. She used to come here a long time ago. She's a little mixed up. Thank you."

Ms. Michaels seemed satisfied and left. A few minutes later, housekeeping arrived with two toothbrushes.

"Dodo," Cricket said, "I'm tired."

"Oh, poor sweetheart, you must be. Take a sleep. I will join you. We can go to the museum later."

Thank heavens, Cricket thought, and they each climbed aboard their ship of a bed. Cricket hoped their sleep would last a long time.

22

BARNEYS

Dodo woke in very good spirits. She didn't seem to remember the incident with hotel security and Cricket didn't bring it up. They'd slept in. Now they both got dressed. Dodo ordered coffee and pastries. Cricket had never been served coffee by her parents. She drank a whole cup with cream and lots of sugar and didn't tell Dodo that Bunny wouldn't approve. They left and went shopping. Dodo was determined to get some clothes.

Barneys was just a block away from the Pierre. It had a doorman, too. A man in a black suit opened the front door the moment they arrived. He barely made eye contact with either of them, but Dodo said, "Why, thank you," as though he'd been waiting all morning just to hold the door for her.

Cricket was beginning to see that her grandmother loved attention from men (even when the men were women, like last night). All kinds of men: butchers, handymen, bellhops, and now the Barneys doorman.

Cricket thought the doorman was more interested in his walkie-talkie than he was in anything or anyone. It seemed old-fashioned of Barneys to give out walkie-talkies. Maybe they were less expensive than cell phones.

Dodo walked through the main floor, touching everything she could get her hands on. She marveled over each bangle, belt, hat, purse, and scarf like the merchandise was part of an interactive museum exhibit. She was in heaven. Cricket was very happy that her grandmother was happy again. The scare from the suitcase robbery must have passed.

It was only eleven-thirty in the morning, but Barneys was full of women Bunny's age. Probably the very same women who would go to the August fund-raising gala in the Hamptons. Cricket bet she'd heard her parents complain about half the women in here. They drifted from counter to counter as though they had all the time in the world to shop. Bunny said that looking good was their vocation. They were always photographed at charity events and they wanted to look better than the people they were photographed with and they wanted to look better than they looked last time they were photographed with them. Bunny said they spent buckets of money on shoes and dresses and jewelry because everything they bought was a tax deduction.

Bunny—poor, poor Bunny. Because of her job she needed to seem rich even though she wasn't rich. She needed to look great but never better than the people with the money. While all the women dressed up at the summer gala in their most special gowns, Bunny rented her dresses every year. Her mother was like Cinderella. At the end of every party her carriage turned back into a pumpkin.

The hair on Cricket's arms was standing up and her glasses were fogging over because the air-conditioning was on full blast. All the salespeople were wearing jackets. They were dressed for December instead of June. She could never work here.

"Dodo," Cricket said, wiping her glasses on her T-shirt, "aren't you cold?"

"Yes, I'm freezing. It's freezing in here."

"Barneys is probably responsible for most of the polar

bears dying off. Think how much energy and fuel and emissions and stuff would be conserved if this store alone just raised the temperature a little bit."

"Cricket, have you been to Japan?"

"No," Cricket said, smiling. "Not yet." Cricket greatly appreciated Dodo allowing the possibility that she had been to Japan.

"In Japan, they've done what you're saying. They are very formal people, the Japanese. But to help with carbon emissions they mandated all government buildings maintain an indoor temperature of eighty-two degrees in the summer. The professional dress code was adapted. No one wears suit jackets in the summer. Tomorrow we should go shopping in Japan."

"Do you think I will like Japan?"

"Japan is wonderful," Dodo said. "What's not to like?"

The salespeople flocked around the charity crowd but steered clear of Dodo. Maybe Cricket hadn't gotten all the dirt off her shirt when she'd washed it in the sink with the nice shampoo last night. Cricket was never taken seriously in stores either. "Never Taken Seriously: The Cricket Cohen Story." She really hoped she could remember that title.

"Do you want a salesperson, Dodo?"

"No one likes old people, Cricket. Not even me. I told

you that. The older you get, the less people see you. Unless you have cancer. Everybody respects a person with cancer. When Dodie got cancer," Dodo said, "everyone rallied around. They were mad. They were furious. They were outraged. Cancer is something to fight. Old age? Forget it. You're on your own and you're not supposed to bother anybody with your complaints. No one considers old age an illness. Old age is like a person with bad luck. Everyone avoids you. Like it's contagious . . . It is very sad, because everyone gets old."

Maybe Dodo was right. When Bunny talked about her father during his cancer, she commended his courage. She was proud he'd enjoyed the end of his life, traveling and eating great food. She'd wanted him to live it up until the last possible moment. She'd told Cricket she was happy that he and Dodo had traveled as long as they could. On the other hand, when Bunny talked about Dodo, she didn't mention bravery. She was more inclined to see Dodo as a nuisance. Dodo didn't get encouragement to do what she loved. In fact, Bunny took Dodo away from everything she loved, everything that had defined her. Instead of respect, Dodo got the calendar.

"Cricket, I collect these scarves. I'm wearing that one, see? With the horse stirrups, that's a classic," Dodo said. She was in front of a circular display case.

Cricket wondered how a salesperson got behind it. There must be a hidden opening somewhere.

"Maybe one day you'll choose one for yourself. From my drawer, if you like." Dodo stared into the glass like Cricket wanted to stare at the fish in the aquarium.

Barneys had a sensational aquarium, according to Dodo. Cricket pretended to appreciate the scarves so that she could leave her grandmother to see the fish without feeling guilty.

The fish were just on the other side of the big room with the scarf display. Behind a wall of glass the neutral tones of high-end shopping were replaced by a brightly colored paradise of coral and fish the colors of peacocks. They were magnificent, gliding and swirling, weaving their way in and out and around the waving seaweed. And because it was Barneys and not a diorama at the Museum of Natural History, diamond rings and gold bracelets and jeweled necklaces hung from each piece of coral. The whole thing was so magical it almost made Cricket like jewelry.

She'd thought it was pretty glamorous to check into a hotel in the middle of the day in your own city, but what a life for a fish, swimming on the Upper East Side of Manhattan among sapphires and emeralds and twenty-two-karat gold. She wished she were in there. She loved swimming. And it had to be warmer in there. Tropical fish needed warm water.

A salesperson came by with a key and opened a lock. Cricket waited for all the water and all the fish to flood the floor.

But the salesperson was able to open a glass window and reach into a very dry display. She removed a necklace from a piece of coral, put it on a black velvet board, and locked the window. Cricket went closer to figure the whole thing out. It was so simple, she felt like an idiot. There were two tanks. A dry one, filled with coral and jewelry, and a wet one filled with plants and fish and the water. The whole thing was like a science-fiction world where children were exhibited behind glass. They appeared to play on jungle gyms in front of ice cream trucks. But they were alone in glass cages. She wanted to run home and write it down.

Dodo joined her for a minute but soon lost interest and moved on. Cricket stayed. The fish were so beautiful and lived such compromised lives. It was upsetting.

"Oh, Cricket, look!" Dodo said from across the way. "I found my shawl. Isn't it wonderful? I'm not cold anymore. Let's go for lunch."

They'd just had breakfast. But Cricket wasn't about to argue.

"You bought one like the one you lost?" Cricket asked.

"Look!" Dodo said. She held up a shawl that was lavender and yellow. Cricket didn't remember ever seeing one like it. Was this like the one that Dodo thought Abby had taken? Was Dodo pretending?

"This is it!" Dodo repeated. "I'm so glad. We will have to tell the security people at the hotel. This is like a treasure hunt."

Cricket tore herself away from the fish.

"Where did you find it?" Cricket said.

"A saleslady was showing it to another woman and she didn't want it but I was delighted to find it. It would have looked awful on her. These are my colors."

Cricket was glad that a salesperson had finally helped Dodo with something. That was why they'd come, after all, to go shopping.

They went across the floor, past the handbags, to the elevator bank and stood next to another man with a walkie-talkie. These guys in the dark suits with the walkie-talkies were everywhere. Cricket thought she'd enjoy using a walkie-talkie and learning all the walkie-talkie lingo: *ten-four*, *copy*, *roger*, and all that. The man with the walkie-talkie entered the elevator with them.

Cricket pushed 9, and he pushed 8. Maybe if she got a walkie-talkie and was dressed warmly, like in a turtleneck sweater, and she got to hang out by the fish, she could work in Barneys. Maybe she would work here, get the keys, and sneak in one night and set all the fish free.

23

WHAT HAPPENED AT THE RESTAURANT

The man with the walkie-talkie got out on the eighth floor and Dodo waved goodbye. When the elevator doors opened on the ninth floor, the smell of grilled meats made Cricket hungry again. She discovered a text from Bunny: How are you and how is the essay? Bunny didn't like being ignored. As Cricket was deciding whether to return the text, the battery died. She tried to think of something else, like the soothing sound of ice cubes tinkling against glassware.

The hostess led them to a table by the window, where they had a view of Madison Avenue below. Moments later a parade of service began. One man brought menus, another man filled their water glasses. An entirely different man arrived with a basket of bread and asked Cricket to select a roll, and when she did he used a set of tongs to place it delicately on her plate. When the waitress came to take their order Dodo ordered a cheese omelet.

"The same, please," Cricket said.

"Cricket," Dodo said quietly as soon as the waitress left, "did you notice the gentleman in the elevator? In the dark suit?"

"With the walkie-talkie?"

"Yes!" Dodo helped herself to some butter and spread it thickly on her roll. "He's quite handsome. He's following us. Don't look now, but he's over by the door."

"Oh, Dodo!" Cricket said. She looked over to the door and sure enough there was a man with a walkie-talkie. But she was pretty sure it wasn't the same man. There were men with walkie-talkies all over the store.

"I don't get out much. Who knows what would happen if I did? He's less than half my age. I mean, it's a little inappropriate. But I guess when you've got it, you've got it!" Dodo winked. She wrapped herself tighter in her new shawl.

Cricket didn't think any of the men in the dark suits

were handsome or following them, but Dodo was enjoying the idea so much; why spoil it by contradicting her?

"You've got it all right," Cricket said. "Your shawl is nice, too." Cricket helped herself to butter with the little butter knife.

"I thought I'd never see this shawl again. That was some trip we took. He died a month later, you know. Here's to Dodie." Dodo raised her water glass and so did Cricket.

"I wish I'd gotten to know him," Cricket said. But as she said it she thought that if she had, she would have also known a different version of her grandmother. The wifely version. The docile version. The version who followed a man, not a woman who led the way.

The waiter arrived with two beautiful omelets and, more important, two glorious metal cones lined with napkins, filled to the brim with french fries, with little pots of mayonnaise on the side. Dodo clapped. So did Cricket.

"It's just like Belgium! They never use ketchup on their fries," Dodo said, taking three fries at once and dipping them. "Oh my goodness. I am in heaven. Your grandfather was part of a big panel in Belgium. We ate in the most wonderful restaurants," Dodo said, "and your grandfather, that remarkable scientist, squirted ketchup all over everything. Can you imagine? He was terrific. But the ketchup."

There they were at a restaurant above Madison Avenue talking about the shame of ketchup like a couple of very fancy ladies. But Dodo would have been just as happy, had they not almost been killed by a roller skater, to be eating hot dogs from a cart in the park. She was versatile that way.

The light outside shifted. A big cloud had moved over the sun. Cricket wondered where her parents were right then and if they'd settled on a house. Her mother had been confident about some place they were seeing this morning. She didn't want to think about it. She glanced at her now-dead phone and took a bite of her omelet. She replayed yesterday. She'd brought Dodo breakfast. Dodo had seemed sad. She didn't like getting old. She missed Dodie. She said she wanted to run away. Cricket left the house with Dodo to have an adventure. She hadn't really thought it through beyond that.

Exactly, her father would say when he finally reached her, *you didn't think.*

Oh, Cricket, her mother would say, *either your phone is charged at all times or it isn't. The reasons are not important. What is important is that you didn't do the simple thing that we asked of you.*

Oh, Cricket, what are we going to do with you?

"How's your omelet?" Dodo asked. "Cricket, are you there?"

"Amazing," Cricket said. "How is yours?"

"Just wonderful."

Hoping her grandmother wouldn't notice, Cricket reached for the elegant little single-serving ketchup bottle in the condiment basket next to the salt and pepper shakers. She wanted to dip a few french fries in something other than mayonnaise. But she wanted to do it as discreetly as possible.

"You are certainly your grandfather's granddaughter," Dodo said, catching her. "Will you excuse me? I'm going to the ladies' room."

Dodo had a little trouble getting up from the table at first. But eventually she figured out how to use the arms of her chair for leverage.

"See, byself! I did it," Dodo said. She wove her way through the dining room and all the women who resembled Bunny, dressed in thousands of shades of tasteful neutral.

Cricket looked outside at all the bright green leaves. Maybe this summer would be better than she'd assumed. Dodo would be coming with them to the

Hamptons, since she didn't have an aide anymore. They could hide out and watch all the Bette Davis movies Cricket hadn't seen yet. During all the boring fund-raising parties, they could pretend to be international spies and prepare dossiers on the guests. The next day they could raid the refrigerator together, digging up giant ziplock bags of leftovers. Maybe they'd eat blinis on the deck or feed cheese to the seagulls. It would be nice to have some company. Maybe she'd figure out a way to get Veronica invited, too. Dodo liked Veronica, even if Bunny didn't.

A table nearby was vacated, and a busboy cleared plates. He probably made less money in a day than the people who left had spent on lunch, Cricket thought. The world was filled with unfairness like that.

Dodo wasn't back, so Cricket went to check up on her. She almost bumped into Dodo's supposed boyfriend standing outside the restaurant, walkie-talkie pressed to his ear. Maybe these guys really did find Dodo attractive after all.

The bathroom was modern, uncluttered, beige, and empty. Cricket didn't see Dodo.

"Dodo?" Cricket called. Where could her grandmother be?

"Cricket?" Dodo said. "I was hoping you'd come! I can't get up." Cricket followed the voice until she saw Dodo's feet under the door of the stall at the end of the long row.

"Are you okay?" Cricket asked. "Should I come in?"

"I think you better," Dodo said, laughing. "I can't get up." Cricket tried the door, but it was locked. Three women walked in and began applying makeup at the mirror. Cricket went into the stall next to Dodo's, hoping they wouldn't notice her wriggling on the floor under the divider. If they did notice, at least she wouldn't be able to see the expressions on their faces. Nothing short of horror-stricken, probably. Bunny certainly wouldn't want her daughter facedown on the floor of a public bathroom.

Dodo laughed when Cricket emerged in her stall.

"Hello!" Cricket said. "So what's going on?"

"I can't get up," Dodo whispered cheerfully.

"Hmm," Cricket said.

"I'd like to get up and go have a cup of coffee." Dodo reached out her right hand and Cricket grabbed on.

"I just need to lean on you," Dodo said. But the angle was wrong and Dodo's underpants were around her ankles, which created other challenges.

Cricket crouched down and wedged her hands into

Dodo's armpits and tried to hoist her up. Dodo rose for a second before she landed back down on the toilet with a thump.

Cricket and Veronica used to spend hours, probably entire days, playing a game like this. Cricket had an enormous stuffed tiger that she and Veronica tried to lift onto Cricket's top bunk. They were little, like four years old, so they always collapsed under the weight of the huge animal. But trying and failing to get the big animal onto the top bunk made them laugh till they could barely breathe. They did it over and over. At the moment, Dodo was the tiger and Cricket found the situation hilarious. She hadn't laughed this hard in a long time.

Eventually Cricket got Dodo (and her underwear) up. It was such an accomplishment that they both screamed for joy. They walked out of the stall, triumphant, and were greeted by withering stares.

"My word," Cricket said, adopting an English accent.

She looked at herself in the mirror and wiped tears off her face, ignoring the other women.

No one in the bathroom was the least bit amused.

What a wicked crowd, she thought.

"My word, indeed," Dodo said. "Darling, shall we resume our luncheon?"

24
THE BARNEYS BASEMENT

Cricket was very much in the mood for an ice cream sundae on a brownie—one of her favorite desserts. Dodo had mentioned wanting coffee. But maybe she would order tea, since they were British now.

There were four men waiting outside the bathroom, all with walkie-talkies and all wearing dark suits. One of them said, "Come with us, please."

"Well, my heavens," Dodo said. It was like a dream come true. She winked at Cricket.

Another man herded Cricket like she was a little farm animal. "What is your relationship to this woman?" he asked.

"She's my grandmother," Cricket said. "What is going on?"

No one answered. Had Bunny sent these guys? In addition to walkie-talkies, they all had wires coming out of their shirt collars that must have been connected to some kind of secret speaker that went into their ears. Did they work for the government? Were they part of the CIA? Did they think that Dodo was a spy because of her old-fashioned 1950s sense of style? Were they after Dodo? She'd traveled all over the world, supposedly collecting art for people. Maybe that was a front. Maybe she was really a secret agent and her enemies had finally caught up to her. Dodo's not knowing who or what to trust supported that theory.

Cricket would die if she was mistaken for a spy. She spent most of her time imagining herself as some kind of scientist: an astrophysicist, a doctor, and obviously a geologist, but spy work was amazing. Spies led secret lives. Spies had adventures like crazy. They had incredible equipment, pens that turned into cameras, cars that could fly, shoes that became dangerous weapons.

What if Dodo actually was a spy? Why had that never occurred to Cricket? Her grandmother had spent most of her life jetting around the globe.

Cricket and Dodo were ushered toward the elevators. They passed the restaurant and then Cricket thought they'd gotten into trouble for not paying, but they hadn't finished eating yet. Cricket had no idea what was going on, but she was thrilled when the wall they were now standing in front of whooshed open. They were going into a secret elevator! To a private tarmac somewhere to board Air Force One. She'd seen pictures of that plane. If the president was on board he could ask for anything to eat and they had to make it for him.

Cricket's mind fired on all cylinders, trying to piece together where they were going and what was happening. Dodo, on the other hand, was leaning on the man who had brought her into the elevator as though they were on a date.

When the secret elevator doors opened again they were in a new world where everything was gray. The paint shone like in a school or a hospital or a submarine. They were in the basement of Barneys. Cricket didn't like it down here. There was no aquarium. It smelled like it was cleaned regularly with heavy disinfectant.

They walked down hallways and by countless closed

doors. She tried to memorize the route the men were taking. But they had made so many turns she was disoriented. Were they in trouble for running away? She was in a maze and she'd never find her way out. It was like being spun before your turn at pin the tail on the donkey. No matter how much she tried to memorize where the back end of the donkey picture was located so she'd pin the tail in the right vicinity, when she took off her blindfold, her tail wasn't ever anywhere near where she thought she'd pinned it.

What if she and Dodo were being kidnapped? What if they were mixed up in something dangerous? One of the walkie-talkies was blaring static, like in the subway when they announced unintelligible information about route changes and delays.

They walked forever, blocks underground. If this was a covert criminal operation, it was a big one.

They stopped in front of a pair of uniformed security guards who were behind a counter checking the bags and coats and pockets of employees. One guard discovered a tie loosely hung around a salesman's neck. It still had the price tag on. He said he'd been modeling it for a woman who wanted to see it on a man, and he must have forgotten about it. The guards filled out a form, and they made the salesman fill out a form. Lots of signatures were exchanged. The guards kept the tie. The man was allowed out.

Was this about shoplifting? Had they been brought here because someone thought they'd stolen something? But the guards were only searching Barneys employees. Cricket went back to the kidnapping theory. Except that didn't make sense either because her parents didn't have the money for ransom. Cricket needed to call her mother. But how? Her phone was dead. It was so dead it wouldn't even turn on. There probably wasn't any reception all the way down here, anyway. They were entirely at these people's mercy.

She and Dodo were taken into a windowless room where a half-dead fly buzzed and flopped on the table. A woman, dressed in a dark suit like the men who had escorted them on their trip downstairs, sat behind a desk. She was steely. Young Bette Davis could have played her. Cricket and Dodo were told to sit down. To the right of the woman's desk was a wall of television sets. Every TV played a different part of Barneys.

One of the men spoke to the woman briefly and then all the men left. No one explained anything, so Cricket watched the poor fly as it struggled to ascend. She noticed cameras, one in each corner of the room. Her heart was still racing. Maybe Dodo was an international fine art thief. Maybe she had the original *Mona Lisa* hidden somewhere. And maybe Bunny had accidentally thrown it away when she downsized Dodo's possessions before the move to New York. Maybe they were going to be deported.

"My name is Ms. Diaz," the woman behind the desk said. She showed a Barneys ID. "I'm a security agent here at the store."

"Hello," Dodo said curtly. She was probably disappointed that all her male friends from the elevator had left the room.

"Do you know why you're here?"

"No, I most certainly do not. Where are the other gentlemen?"

"May I have some identification, please?" Agent Diaz said. Cricket hoped Dodo would cooperate. Dodo could be crabby. Especially when she thought she was being ignored. Cricket was relieved when Dodo rummaged in her purse and produced a driver's license.

"California," Agent Diaz said, looking at the license and typing something into a database. "Why do you have an out-of-state ID?"

"I just moved. From Los Alamos."

Agent Diaz looked at Cricket. Cricket wasn't sure if she was supposed to verify what Dodo had just said. Agent Diaz finally said, "ID please."

"Huh?"

"Do you have a state-issued ID?" Agent Diaz said.

"I'm sorry," Cricket said. "I'm eleven."

"Name?" Agent Diaz looked more aggravated.

"Cricket Cohen." She wished her parents had given her a normal name. How embarrassing. If this really was about Dodo's stolen-art ring and Barneys thought Cricket was involved, her name was all wrong. She should be called Lucinda Barrister. She hoped Agent Diaz wouldn't ask for Bunny's name.

"Address?"

"Sixty-four West Sixty-Fourth Street," Cricket answered.

Agent Diaz entered more information and returned Dodo's license.

"Mrs. Fabricant, my men have been following you," the woman said.

"I know that," Dodo said, blushing.

"A few moments ago you indicated you didn't know why you were here," Agent Diaz said.

"Well, I thought it was for romance, but that no longer seems to be the case," Dodo said with a sad smile.

Like the best part of her day was over and all she had left was a lousy ticket stub.

There was a knock on the door and a new agent poked his head in.

"Hello," Dodo said to the man. She waved at him.

"Hello," the man said, somewhat taken aback. He moved closer to Agent Diaz as though she could protect him.

"That is a charming pocket square you're wearing," Dodo said.

"Excuse me?"

"I said, I like your pocket square. It looks very handsome on you."

So this was the plan. Dodo was going to flirt her way out of this mess. Dodo had not taught Cricket how to flirt. But she needn't worry. Dodo always flirted enough for at least two people.

"Mrs. Fabricant," Agent Diaz said, "the reason you're here is that shawl."

"Oh my heavens. Everyone loves this shawl. It's the best thing I ever bought," Dodo said, smiling.

"Do you happen to have the receipt for it, ma'am?" the man asked.

"Don't be ridiculous," Dodo said. "I got it in Florence. Years ago. It was a wonderful trip."

Agent Diaz and the new guy looked at each other.

"Mmhmm," Agent Diaz said.

"I'm going to ask you again. Do you have a receipt for the merchandise?"

"I doubt it. I lost it in the move. I lost everything in the move. Everything's gone," Dodo said.

The man looked at Dodo and shook his head. "You've got to call this in, boss. We've got a confused senior and a minor."

"Excuse me," Cricket said. "Speaking of calls, don't we get a phone call? Do we each get one? I'd like to call my parents."

"Are they local?" Agent Diaz asked. "At the address you gave me?"

"They're on Long Island today." The minute she said that she regretted it. She should have said her parents were very local, as a matter of fact. Then maybe she and Dodo could just promise to go home, and then walk out of here.

"Time to call it in," the man with the pocket square said again.

Cricket didn't want anyone calling anything in. She wanted to do the calling. If ever anyone needed a lawyer, it was now. Where was Richard Cohen, attorney-at-law, when you needed him?

"Please, my phone call," she repeated. If she only had a charged phone she'd have already been dialing.

The smart board behind Agent Diaz's desk came alive with multiple images. Each one was time-stamped with that day's date. The screens showed, from four angles, Dodo Fabricant removing the shawl from the display and putting it around herself. It was right there, many times over. Cricket reached over to feel the shawl. It was remarkably soft. It also still had a Barneys price tag hanging from it.

"Dodo, don't worry, we're going to straighten all this out."

"Oh, I'm not worried. They've made a terrible mistake."

"I need to call my parents," Cricket said again. She impressed herself with how steady her voice was. She was much calmer now that it was clear this wasn't an international art bust.

Agent Diaz handed her a phone receiver. "I'd like to speak with them, too. What's the number?" she asked.

Cricket stared at the base of the phone on the desk. Who should she ask Agent Diaz to dial? Her father was way less high-strung and he was the lawyer. But he rarely answered his phone if he didn't recognize the number. So Cricket recited Bunny's phone number and Agent

Diaz punched it in. While the call went through, Cricket practiced what she'd say.

Hi, Mom, good news! Dodo isn't a spy or an international art thief. But we need you to turn around and come back to the city right away and tell Dad to bring his lawyer briefcase to Barneys.

Bunny's phone went to straight to voice mail. She should have called her father. At the beep she spoke without thinking: "Hi, Mom, it's Cricket. Um, I hope things are going well and give me a call when you can, I guess."

The last thing she wanted to do was leave her mother a message that was too alarming.

She gave the phone back to Agent Diaz, mortified by how she'd bungled her call for help. What was going to happen now? How would her parents find her? What if they did send Dodo up the river? What if Cricket was going to foster care? What if they were so mad at her for not charging her phone they left her there?

All we asked you to do today was write your memoir. Why can't you be responsible, Cricket? Why are you in the basement of Barneys accused of a crime? Oh, Cricket.

She couldn't think about it.

"We have to put you and your grandmother in custody."

"In custody?"

"Until your parents can be reached."

"What if we pay for the shawl?" Cricket offered. Dodo must have enough money in her wallet. Why hadn't anyone thought of this? Surely if they paid, they could go home. She just wanted to get them home.

"Cricket," Dodo said, "I already paid for this shawl. In Florence. And it isn't even clean, Abby's been wearing it."

"I know, Dodo," Cricket said. "You're right. But I was thinking we'd pay for it just to get out of here, and then sort it out later."

"Ah," Dodo said emphatically. "That makes a lot of sense. Let's do that. And we should go upstairs for some coffee and dessert and then we can settle up at the restaurant, too. We'll sort it all out later."

"I still can't release you," Agent Diaz said.

"Why?" Cricket asked. "If we pay, you have no reason to hold us."

"You're a minor and I need to hand you over to a responsible adult. Your grandmother isn't that person right now. I'm sorry."

Cricket looked at Dodo. Dodo was either not paying attention or pretending not to. Either way it was better than Dodo actually responding to the charge of being irresponsible.

"My mother will answer her phone soon, she's probably just somewhere with bad service."

"You can call her again from the precinct. We have to turn you over to protective custody. My associate has already called the police."

Cricket looked up and saw that the other agent was gone. She hadn't noticed that he'd left.

"We aren't dangerous!" Cricket said. Although at the moment she wished they were. Then they could turn the tables. They'd pull out their weapons and jump over the desk and break down the door and run.

"You're a minor. We have to call it in to the local precinct."

"What a shame," Dodo said.

25

OFFICER COOLIDGE AND OFFICER BRYANT

Cricket and Dodo sat on a bench in front of the security desk waiting for their police escort. From her proximity to employees entering and exiting the building, Cricket learned this fun fact: all the Barneys salespeople walked around with transparent plastic pouches to keep personal stuff in, like phones, combs, Chap Stick, wallets. Cricket also learned that the men with the walkie-talkies were all over the store communicating with one another about potential shoplifters. All that stuff was clear, but what still wasn't clear was why she and Dodo were considered dangerous.

"Why are we here?" Dodo asked.

"I have to say, Dodo, I'm not sure either," Cricket said. "But when we get where we're going, I think everything will make more sense." She kicked herself for not taking better care of Dodo.

"I'm sure it will," Dodo said. "You're usually right."

Cricket hoped Dodo wasn't just saying that to make them feel better. Cricket wanted to be the one to do the comforting. She took Dodo's hand.

Five minutes later two uniformed police officers walked in. One was short with a mustache and the other was tall and thinner. Cricket didn't like men with mustaches. Nosy Pete the doorman had a mustache.

"Hey, Taylor," the short one with the mustache said as he high-fived the biggest guy behind the desk.

"Bryant, my man," Taylor said.

"What's with the new hairstyle?"

"You don't like?" The guard ran his hand over his freshly shaved and extremely shiny head, feigning hurt feelings. "I have to say, Bryant, you're looking pretty juicy. You been eating a few extra doughnuts? I do believe there's even more of you to love."

A couple of the other desk guys laughed. Meanwhile the taller officer took a pad from his back pocket and went to Agent Diaz.

"What do we got?" he asked. It seemed like he and Agent Diaz had been through this kind of thing many times. He took notes off to the side.

The short officer entertained a little crowd by the desk.

It seemed like a good sign that no one was in a hurry. In fact, it was all feeling very friendly. Until Cricket saw the guns. The police officers sent to protect her from her confused grandmother both had guns. And handcuffs. She squeezed Dodo's hand. How could Bunny not have answered her phone?

When the note-taking and the stand-up routine were over, both officers came to the bench. The tall one introduced himself first.

"Good afternoon, ladies. My name is Officer Coolidge."

"I'm Officer Bryant," the other one said, extending his arm to Dodo. "Mrs. Fabricant. Would you do me the honor?" Dodo willingly took his arm. She looked relieved. "We are going on a date," Bryant said.

"Well, of course we are," Dodo said. She winked at Cricket.

"I'm Officer Coolidge," the other officer said again.

Cricket had heard him the first time. Was he nervous?

"It's nice to meet you," Officer Coolidge added.

"Hello," Cricket said.

"Your name is Cricket?"

"Yes," Cricket admitted for the second time today. Why hadn't her parents given her a regular name?

"Okay, Cricket. Are you scared?"

"No," she said. Of course she was scared. Duh. But Officer Coolidge smiled, making it clear that his primary intention was to make her feel at ease.

"I just want to make sure you understand what's going on."

"Sort of. Not really," Cricket said. "I'm a minor and my grandmother is confused so we have to wait with you till you reach my parents?"

"That's pretty much the story," Coolidge said.

His manner was calm and kind and Cricket appreciated that.

"We want to keep you both safe. Sound good?"

It didn't sound that good, but Cricket followed him anyway. He was the one with a gun.

She wondered if they were going to walk through the store in police custody, in front of all the shoppers and salespeople. But they walked through another hall and up a short flight of stairs, past a Dumpster full of mannequin legs and arms and heads and torsos, and finally through a door that was just for employees. A small crowd watched as the officers took Dodo and Cricket to the police car. Under different circumstances the novelty of entering a police car with a crowd watching would have thrilled Cricket. But not today. She just wanted to go home.

Officer Bryant opened the back door.

"Oh, man," he said. "Give me a minute." He leaned into the car, rearranging something on the backseat. Cricket hoped there wasn't a bomb back there, or a bunch of other criminals he'd forgotten about. But it was just a backpack and a shopping bag from a children's shoe store. He threw them into the trunk.

"Sorry about that," he said. "There you go. Now there's some room for you." He patted the seat and Dodo climbed in.

She had to scoot across. She wasn't nimble and sliding over made her skirt bunch up. But good sport that she was, she laughed at her own ineptitude.

"Dodo, do you want a little shove?" asked Cricket.

"I think that is exactly what I need, sweetheart."

Cricket climbed in and pushed. It was funny. Hopefully laughing in a police car while in police custody wasn't going to get them in more trouble. Nothing today had gone the right way.

Coolidge got in the driver's seat, radioed something

in, and turned on the ignition. Cricket helped Dodo with her seat belt.

"Mrs. Fabricant?" Officer Bryant leaned over from the front and smiled through the metal screen. "I'm trying to figure out how old you are. I'm usually pretty good with this. So I'm going to say, thirty-five? Forty?"

Cricket could not believe this guy. He was such a snake charmer. He must really think he could get away with anything. He was probably captain of every team in school. Or wanted to be.

"You know perfectly well I am not thirty-five," Dodo said. She touched her hair. "You are a real flirt."

"Amen," Coolidge said. "Amen."

"Let me ask you this then. Can we stop and get you a coffee, a pastry? You ladies hungry?"

Dodo looked at Cricket and Cricket nodded.

"That would be nice," Dodo said. Coffee and dessert was where they had been heading when they'd been intercepted outside the bathroom and, come to think of it, they hadn't finished lunch. How long ago was that? Cricket had no idea what time it was. The officers had a little discussion about where to go and Dodo smiled. It was like they were all on a date.

"Where are you officers taking us?" Dodo asked.

"To the precinct," Coolidge said. He drove across

Sixtieth and pulled up to the curb on First Avenue. Officer Bryant went inside a café.

"The precinct, you were asking, is on Sixty-Seventh Street between Lex and Third. As soon as we get ahold of your daughter, she'll come and pick you up. But in the meantime, you'll keep us company, okay?"

"Well, I don't know," Dodo said. "We had other plans for the rest of the day, didn't we, Cricket?"

"We most certainly did," Cricket said. "But I don't mind going. I've never been to a precinct."

"So you'd like to go, sweetheart?" Dodo asked.

"I bet it will be interesting. Have you ever been inside a precinct?"

"No," Dodo said. "I don't think I have. You want to go?"

"They seem very nice," Cricket said, shrugging her shoulders.

"They do," Dodo agreed. "They really do. And I do like an adventure."

"Me, too," Cricket said.

Dodo leaned forward and said to Coolidge, "We've decided. It's settled. We will go with you."

Cricket thought she'd handled the interaction well, because Dodo thought they were going voluntarily. The only way to improve the day was to make whatever happened from now on seem like it was good for Dodo. Which would be a nice distraction from feeling scared.

Coolidge caught her eye in the rearview mirror and smiled approvingly. Officer Bryant returned to the car with a bag of treats.

Dodo looked out the window of the backseat, like a dog on a long trip.

26
THE NINETEENTH PRECINCT

The patrol car continued north to Sixty-Seventh Street. It pulled up in front of an old-fashioned-looking police station four stories high and wedged between two much taller, newer buildings. The precinct looked like something out of a children's book about progress and new things conquering old things.

Officer Bryant escorted Dodo out of the car while Officer Coolidge came around for Cricket.

"My partner is a real character," he said.

"So is my grandmother," Cricket said.

"She really is. You've got a nice thing with her. I like how you talk to her." He offered Cricket his arm and she took it.

"She's my favorite," Cricket said.

"I can see why," he said.

The minute they walked into the Nineteenth Precinct station house, Cricket had déjà vu. She'd never been to any police station, let alone this one, but the sergeant's desk was located exactly where she remembered it, and the lighting fixtures were familiar. Why? It was driving her crazy. Then Officer Coolidge told them this was the precinct they'd used as a location in the movie *Breakfast at Tiffany's*. Dodo had shown her that movie in California at least three times.

When this whole thing was over, they would have to watch it again.

Officer Bryant sat Dodo on a chair in the waiting area. Cricket sat, too. If it hadn't been for the guns, she'd have almost been happy. But she couldn't get over the guns. All the officers in this building were wearing guns. Guns killed people. Guns were responsible for so many horrible deaths, some accidental, some intentional. Cricket hated guns. Her family hated guns.

"All right," Bryant said. "You're our guests. So please make yourselves comfortable. There's a TV up there,

here's your pastries, your coffee. Coolidge is going to get you some water. I've got to fill out a little bit of paperwork and then try to get ahold of your daughter." He showed Dodo and Cricket a piece of paper. "Is this the right number?"

Dodo didn't say anything so Cricket answered.

"Yes," she said. "Do you want my father's number, too?"

"Sure, why not," Bryant said. "Thank you."

Both officers saluted.

The platform supporting the sergeant's desk was at least a foot high. Everyone and everything on it loomed above the rest of the people in the station. Next to the platform was a gate that separated the public part of station life from the private part. Officers Bryant and Coolidge went through that locked gate when they said goodbye. Everything behind the gate was obviously where the real police stuff happened. Cricket hoped she wouldn't end up back there. But she also really wanted to know what it was like.

The sergeant's area faced the TV and the front door. His desk was an island, the circumference of which was a low wooden shelf covered with piles of forms in different baskets. Cricket could see over the gate. Bryant was back there filling out one of those forms. The sergeant lived on his island with three other people who answered phones and sent out dispatches over their computers.

A girl listening to headphones walked in the front door. She looked like a dancer. Her hair was piled up on her head in a topknot and her T-shirt was falling off one shoulder. At first Cricket thought they were about the same age. But she said hello to the sergeant, he buzzed her in, and she walked through the gate. She was a police officer! What if Cricket was a police officer? Would she be a detective? A forensics expert? Was that girl an undercover cop? Cricket wished the girl hadn't disappeared. She wanted to follow her.

But she was on this side of the island, where a golf match on TV was her entertainment. Golf was probably the most boring game invented. A police precinct, however, was nothing but excitement. A man came in off the street and approached the island. He wanted to file a complaint about a stolen car. A few minutes later a cop car pulled up out front and two officers walked in with a man in handcuffs. Cricket tried to pay very close attention.

The prisoner looked angry. Or maybe he was in pain. He winced. Maybe it was the handcuffs? They must hurt. A lot. She tried not to look as he walked past her. Was he a criminal? Had he been falsely accused? Was he violent? Maybe he was like her and Dodo and hadn't done anything. One officer and the man passed through the gate.

The other officer placed a cell phone, a wallet, a pack of gum, and a book of matches on the sergeant's desk. Cricket guessed they had been taken from the prisoner. The sergeant picked each item up, described it out loud, and noted it on another form before placing each thing in an envelope.

It was just like on TV. Next the officer joined his partner in the back and led the guy down the hall to a room that was behind a large window. Cricket strained to see what was going on in there. It looked like his fingerprints were being taken. She saw another officer take something, a key maybe, from a desk. Then he opened up a cell that was along the back wall. She watched the man get locked up. She was terrified. Would she and Dodo end up in that cell? What if the man who was already in the cell didn't like them? Were there separate cells somewhere else for women and children?

Officer Coolidge returned a few minutes later with two bottles of water and some napkins.

"How are we doing?"

"Did someone just get arrested?" Cricket asked. All the color had left her face.

"It happens," Coolidge said. "Are you okay?"

"I don't know. I guess so. Yes." Cricket wanted to be courageous.

"It's all good, don't worry. My partner got hold of your mother and she was already heading home with your father. They should be here soon. In the meantime, can I bring you anything else? Crayons? I got crayons. But you don't strike me as the crayon type. Cards?"

Cricket was afraid to ask what was going to happen to the man in the cell. She really hoped that when Bunny came, they'd be allowed to go home and it would all be over.

"So what do you say? A deck of cards?"

"Dodo, want to play gin?"

"Yes! I love gin. That would be great."

"We'd love some cards. Thank you," Cricket said.

And Officer Coolidge said he'd be right back. Cricket hoped she'd sounded casual because if they did get locked up, it would be better to have a deck of cards than to not have one.

"I'm going to the bathroom," Cricket said.

"All right," Dodo said. "I'll wait right here like a good person."

Cricket hoped that the bathroom would be behind the gate. And it was. She got buzzed in and walked by the part of the sergeant's desk where the officer had filled out all the forms, and then she walked by the room that the holding cell was in. There was just a plate of glass separating her from that room. There was an actual person behind bars in there. She couldn't get over it. The bathroom wasn't much farther down the hall. Cricket hurried. Turned out she didn't like being on this side of the gate after all.

27
MISSING

The gate buzzed and Cricket returned to her original spot in the waiting area. Dodo wasn't there. Cricket asked an officer behind the desk if he'd seen an older woman leave.

"Nope, maybe she went to the bathroom," he said, and went back to his paperwork. Cricket had just come from the bathroom. Dodo wasn't there. Dodo had run away. Like she always did. Except this time they weren't playing together. Cricket wasn't accustomed to being on the opposite team. Maybe this was what Abby had felt like, being tricked constantly.

Why had Dodo done this to her? She had to find her. And ideally before Coolidge came back with the playing cards. If they hadn't planned on locking them up in a holding cell, maybe they'd change their minds now. It couldn't be good to be running from the cops. *Oh, Dodo, what were you thinking?*

When she thought the desk sergeant was distracted, Cricket walked outside. She was careful to stay on the left of the front window so no one inside could see her. Cricket looked down the block. Lexington Avenue was busy with cars and traffic and buses and people. If only Dodo weren't wearing such a neutral-colored coat. She didn't see Dodo. She turned and looked the other way, toward Third Avenue. At the corner was a shawarma cart. And lo and behold, Dodo was in front, paying for a sandwich. Cricket ran.

Dodo hailed a cab. Cricket imagined hailing another cab and then saying, "Follow that taxi!" What was she going to do? She didn't have any money to get her own cab. She ran faster and reached the corner before Dodo had gotten all the way into the taxi.

"Dodo, where are you going?" Cricket asked, trying to catch her breath.

"To the airport. Are you coming?"

"Oh, Dodo. Please come back to the precinct with me. Let's wait for Bunny and my dad."

"Driver, the airport."

"Dodo, I really don't want you to do that."

"Why are you trying to stop me? Let me close the door. Driver, let's go."

The driver was a young woman who didn't seem to like conflict. She stared straight ahead.

"Dodo, please don't leave me here. Come out. I want to talk to you."

When they had run away earlier, she'd thought they were playing a game. It didn't seem like Dodo was playing a game now.

"Dodo, I'm scared. Please come."

The driver looked at Dodo from the rearview mirror. "Hello? Are we going to the airport? LaGuardia or Kennedy? I don't have all day."

"Just a minute, I'm thinking," Dodo said, clearly getting more and more mixed up by the second.

Cricket saw her chance. "Dodo, just come out for a minute and we can catch another cab."

"Oh, all right."

Cricket helped her out of the taxi and the taxi sped away up Third Avenue with Dodo's shawarma.

"I'm so turned around, where are we?" Dodo said when they reached the sidewalk.

"We're in New York City. We're together and we are going to be okay. I love you, Dodo," Cricket said.

"I love you too, sweetheart."

"Don't worry, Dodo."

"I'm sorry."

"You don't have to be sorry about anything. And please don't be scared. Everything is going to be fine. I promise."

Cricket didn't normally go around making promises. But the most important thing seemed to be making Dodo feel better, and she did think she could do that. "I think we have treats waiting for us at the precinct. Can we go back?"

They started back toward the station and Cricket saw Coolidge and Bryant, who must have been watching them from up the block. Fleeing from the police was bad. She'd never forgive herself if Dodo had traded escape for worse punishment at the precinct.

But when they walked in the door, Coolidge just smiled and led them back to their seats.

The bag of treats Officer Bryant had given them was still unopened on the bench. Maybe if they were put in that cell, they'd take these things away from them. She opened the bag and found a coffee, a smoothie, and a chocolate-chip cookie. She took out Dodo's cup of coffee and put two sugars in. She stirred and checked to make sure it wasn't too hot before giving it to Dodo.

"Cricket, what are we doing here?"

"Well, believe it or not, we got in a little situation at Barneys and now we're waiting for Mom, for Bunny. Then we're going home, right?" Cricket said. She looked at Officer Coolidge, afraid he wasn't going to corroborate. She really hoped what she was saying was true.

"Yes, indeed," he said.

Cricket was ecstatic. They weren't getting locked up. She took out the huge chocolate-chip cookie Bryant had bought and put it on a napkin for Dodo.

"What kind of situation?" Dodo asked, holding her cookie.

"A misunderstanding. We had a misunderstanding with someone at Barneys. But it's all worked out."

"That's exactly right, there was a misunderstanding, Mrs. Fabricant. But you don't need to worry about anything. Your granddaughter's got the whole thing under control and I bet Officer Bryant will be back soon. He's taken quite a shine to you. I'm going in the back to get those cards."

"Thank you," Cricket said. She wanted to hug him. He left through the little gate. He walked down the hall, past the room where the other officers had locked up the man. So far she and Dodo had been lucky. They hadn't even been handcuffed. They'd been fed. The officers were treating them like they were good people who had gotten themselves into a mix-up.

"This is some adventure, Cricket," Dodo said.

"You can say that again," said Cricket.

28

THE WAITING GAME

Officer Coolidge brought out a deck of cards and a stool, which he set up for Cricket and Dodo in the waiting area like a card table. He also brought over a notebook and a pen in case they wanted to keep score.

"Don't cheat," he said, smiling, "or we'll have to bust you."

Cricket shuffled and dealt the cards. The sound of the cards fluttering past one another was very comforting. Cricket arranged her hand the way Dodo had taught her. All the cards of the same suit went next to one another first. She put all her spades together, and then all her hearts. She had two clubs and a pair of diamond face cards. Lastly, she arranged her cards in order of their value.

Dodo picked up her cards.

"Do you want to go first?" Cricket asked.

"What?"

"Do you want to go first?"

"Yes, I did. I wanted to go first," Dodo said. She put her cards down and wiped her eyes. She was crying. Cricket put her cards down and put her arms around her grandmother.

She took Dodo's hand. It was old and oddly soft, covered with giraffe spots from the sun. Dodo's fingers were thick and twisty and gnarled like tree roots.

Cricket caught the sergeant looking at her. She couldn't read his expression, but he made her nervous. People in charge usually did.

She looked around in Dodo's purse and found some hand lotion. She squeezed some out and rubbed it into Dodo's hands. Dodo used to do that for her. They'd set up a spa in the bathroom and do each other's nails and give each other hand massages.

Dodo willingly turned one hand over and Cricket pressed on her grandmother's palm with her thumbs.

She worked her way out from the middle of Dodo's hand to the ends of her fingers. Dodo closed her eyes.

"Oh, Cricket, I wanted to go first. How did I end up here instead?"

Cricket wasn't sure how to answer. Did Dodo mean how did she end up in the Nineteenth Precinct, or in New York City, or old?

"Life, I guess," Cricket said. That seemed like the right answer.

"Yes, life. I can't keep it all organized. It's too long. Will Bunny be mad at me?"

"No," Cricket said. "You didn't do anything wrong."

"Yes, I did. I got old. I am a burden."

"Dodo. You're a person. You are not a burden. Everyone gets old. They have to."

"I wanted to be different. I wanted to be the exception," Dodo said, smiling.

She looked wise again. Like she had a complete grip on her predicament.

Cricket imagined that the inside of Dodo's mind would be dented and scarred. Marks left from the people and the things she missed; imprints, created by loss. Dodo had lost her husband. She had lost her youth. Now she was losing her independence.

Two new officers walked in the front door leading

another handcuffed man. They walked right by Dodo and Cricket. Cricket squeezed Dodo's hand.

The cuffs were scary.

Officer Bryant reappeared. Cricket was very glad to see him.

"How are we doing? Everything okay? My boys treating you well?"

Dodo perked up at the sight of her gentleman friend. So did Cricket.

"We just saw another criminal," Cricket whispered.

"Well. Not everyone we bring in here is as classy as you ladies."

"What will happen to that young man?" Dodo asked.

Bryant looked over at the prisoner behind the gate, who was being fingerprinted, and shook his head. "I don't know, he's not my collar. But I'm sure he'll get what he deserves. I see my partner brought you the good cards. Did he tell you we reached your daughter, Mrs. Fabricant? She's on her way."

"Yes, he did," Dodo said. She dug in her purse and put on some lipstick.

"All right then, I'm gonna go back to my desk and if I don't get called out, I'll be here when she arrives. I'd like to meet her, to tell you the truth."

He left and Dodo fussed with her hair and fixed the

collar of her coat. The boring golf program continued on the TV. Cricket remembered the shawl from Barneys and wondered what had happened to it. Barneys must have kept it. She was about to ask Dodo where it was when Bunny burst through the front door. Cricket wanted to yell after Officer Bryant, "My mother, my mother is here. Please come back!"

29

BUNNY'S BIG MOMENT

Bunny flew into the precinct repeating "Oh my God" over and over so many times Cricket wondered if she'd ever hear her mother say anything else. Finally she asked what had happened and if they were all right. She hugged Cricket so tightly she could barely breathe.

"Where's Daddy?" Cricket gasped. He was the lawyer, after all.

"He's parking the car. What happened? Where is your phone? I tried to reach you all morning. Cricket, you've got to answer your phone!"

In all the excitement of nearly being sent up the river, being part of an international spy ring, going in a police car, and watching criminals be booked and processed, Cricket had forgotten that this part was coming. The Bunny part. The part where she got in trouble for not having a charged cell phone and not doing as instructed. She found herself thanking some invisible force above when the sergeant called out from his island.

"Mrs. Fabricant?" he said.

Dodo, Cricket, and Bunny looked over. Then up. Cricket pushed her mother toward the sergeant. She had to answer him, it was the law.

"Do you mean Mrs. Cohen, officer, or Mrs. Fabricant?" Bunny asked. "I'm Mrs. Cohen, Mrs. Fabricant is my mother."

"I apologize," the sergeant said. "Mrs. Cohen. Mrs. Fabricant, you're good. Mrs. Cohen, why don't you step up over here, please?"

Now that Bunny was here, she'd have to do the talking. Dodo and Cricket could relax, finally. Maybe they'd get back to their card game. They had half a cookie left, too.

"How was your drive in, Mrs. Cohen?" Cricket heard the sergeant ask her. She knew that Bunny hated this kind of small talk when she was tense.

"Fine," Bunny answered. "No, it wasn't. Discovering that my mother and my daughter were being held up in a police precinct was very stressful. Luckily we were already halfway to the city when we got the call. I don't understand why they were brought here. Shoplifting, the officer said on the phone?"

"You're upset."

"Yes, I am! I'm very upset."

"I hear that. Let me talk you through the day's events, Mrs. Cohen. This hasn't happened before?"

"No!" Bunny said incredulously. "My mother is a lot of things, but she has the money to buy whatever she wants, why would she be shoplifting? She isn't a shoplifter. Where are the arresting officers? I demand to speak to the people who are responsible for this."

When Bunny didn't like what someone was telling her, she accused them of patronizing her. So did Dodo, come to think of it.

"Mrs. Cohen, let's have the officers in question come up here and walk you through what happened. We're going to work this out. We're here to help, I promise." He picked up his phone and called for Coolidge and Bryant.

Cricket felt bad for her father. He was probably driving around in circles and feeling really tense about how the minute he walked in he was going to get an earful from Bunny about how long it had taken him to find a parking space.

The gate opened and Officers Bryant and Coolidge entered the waiting area. Dodo was focusing on her cards. She discarded a jack of hearts. Cricket picked up her grandmother's discard and went through the motions of her card game, but truthfully she wasn't paying much attention. She'd gladly lose every hand if it meant she could continue to eavesdrop on what Bunny and her new friends the police were saying.

"Hello, Mrs. Cohen?" Bryant said, extending his hand and introducing himself. Cricket saw Bunny take notice of his mustache immediately. She hated mustaches, too. "I'm Officer Bryant, and this is my partner, Officer Coolidge."

They all shook hands. Since Coolidge was taller and the more polished of the two, Cricket was sure her mother preferred him.

"Hello," Bunny said. She looked over at Cricket, who quickly went back to her card game and discarded a two of clubs.

"How was your drive?" Officer Coolidge asked.

"It's a beautiful day for driving," Officer Bryant said.

Cricket knew there were only so many times Bunny could answer the asinine question about her drive into town before she blew her top. "Can you please explain to me why my mother and my daughter were brought here?" Bunny said.

Officer Coolidge took the blue pad out of his back pants pocket. He flipped through his notes—Cricket was surprised how many pages—until he got to the beginning.

"At 12:43 p.m.," he said, "your mother, Mrs. Fabricant, was apprehended by security at Barneys. She was wearing a shawl not yet paid for."

"Apprehended? My goodness."

"She was wearing merchandise she hadn't paid for."

"Maybe she was going to pay for it," Bunny said, looking over at Dodo.

Dodo kept her eyes on her cards.

"According to the security footage, she had been wearing the shawl for over an hour and had eaten lunch in the restaurant with the shawl."

"But she hadn't left the store," Bunny said.

"Correct. That is true. But each store is responsible for setting its own policy, and Barneys's store policy is that once unpaid merchandise is removed from its original department, the store has the authority to detain the person who removed it. This was the case with your mother."

"So," Bunny said, trying to follow, "my mother took this shawl from the main floor to the ninth floor? Why would she do that? She loves shopping. She has a Barneys charge card. What you're saying doesn't make any sense."

"Yes, ma'am." Coolidge looked through his notes.

"If she was shoplifting she would have hidden the shawl, wouldn't she? Isn't that what shoplifters do?" Bunny looked around, wondering where on earth her husband was.

"I understand it's hard to wrap your head around this," Officer Coolidge said. "Your mother was very insistent that the shawl was hers. This was when we were called in."

Now Richard, clearly agitated, walked in the door of the precinct. He hugged Cricket and kissed Dodo. Cricket wondered if he lingered there to avoid the wrath that was about to be unleashed by Bunny.

"Oh my God. Richard!" Bunny said. They embraced like they had been separated by a world war and at least five life-changing misunderstandings. They reminded Cricket of characters from one of Dodo's movies.

Richard addressed the officers. "I'm Richard Cohen," he said.

He was still squeezing Bunny tightly. As a lawyer, Richard had had some dealings with the police. He'd once represented a friend who'd gotten into some trouble. He said the most important thing was not letting things escalate. Cricket didn't trust her mother not to let things escalate. Bunny usually fired first and thought later. She was a loose cannon.

Officer Bryant and Officer Coolidge introduced themselves to Richard.

"I was just going over the events of this morning with your wife," Coolidge said.

"Don't let me interrupt," Richard said.

"Well, as I was just explaining to your wife, your mother-in-law was confused at Barneys."

"Confused?" Richard asked. "Now I'm confused. I'm sorry to interrupt. But was shoplifting involved or not?"

"Good question. As I was explaining, Mrs. Fabricant took a shawl from a display on the main floor to the ninth floor. She wore this item to lunch and to the bathroom. She did not pay for it. She was apprehended by security and asked to produce a receipt. She said that she had no receipt because she had bought the shawl in Italy many years ago."

"Were charges brought?" Richard asked.

"Yes, were there charges brought?" Bunny asked, beaming. She smiled at Richard like he was the most intelligent man on earth.

"No. The store chose not to press charges."

"Then why are they here? Why were my mother-in-law and daughter brought here? If there aren't any charges, why were they arrested?"

"They haven't been arrested," Officer Bryant said. "They've been kept here until we could find a responsible party to whom we could release them. Mr. and Mrs. Cohen, coming to terms with the confusion of a loved one can be very upsetting. It's a lot to process."

"Gin," Dodo said to Cricket. She turned one card facedown on the stool and displayed her winning hand. Three queens, four fours, and a five, six, and seven of spades.

Cricket collected the cards and put them in a pile to shuffle. She'd probably lose the next hand, too. She was too busy eavesdropping on Coolidge's account of the events. He spoke in a very level tone.

"Would you like to sit down?" Bryant said.

"You want to take a break before we continue? Can I bring you something cold to drink?" Officer Coolidge asked.

"I don't need to take a break," Bunny said. "I don't want something cold to drink."

Richard placed his hand on Bunny's shoulder, but she shrugged him off. If only she knew how hostile she sounded when she was this upset. Richard knew it was best to tread lightly.

Cricket dealt a new hand while the sergeant leaned over the bull pen and suggested they all have a seat by the window. The four of them relocated to a bench in front of the window, a few feet away from Cricket and Dodo.

Maybe because she was now visible from the street, Bunny pulled herself together almost immediately.

"How we doing? It's a lot to process. I know. My mother has Alzheimer's," Officer Bryant said.

"Alzheimer's! What does that have to do with anything?" Bunny snapped.

Everyone seemed a little surprised by her outburst. Even she looked a little surprised. She never lost control in public.

"But I'm sorry about your mother," Bunny added, as if she could recolor the shade of her earlier aggression.

Dodo was either not paying attention to their conversation or pretending not to. Cricket would put money on the latter. People were talking about her as if she weren't there or wouldn't understand. It was awkward. It actually was patronizing and by listening, Cricket felt like she was betraying Dodo a little. Everyone was talking about Dodo a few feet away from Dodo, saying things she didn't think Dodo would like to hear.

"Thank you, Mrs. Cohen," said Officer Bryant. He was graciously going to let Bunny's rudeness go. "It's a hard thing to accept, believe me. I fought it for a long time. My mother had it for about ten years before we really knew. But once me and my brothers did get the diagnosis, I have to say, life got a little easier. You know, the person does weird things and you kind of write it off as part of their personality or whatever. But when you realize later that they couldn't actually help it, well, you feel bad."

Dodo put her cards down and looked around in her purse. She found her mirror and started fussing with her hair again. It was like she was about to lose something fundamental and she was surrendering. But her appearance wasn't something she'd let anyone take away. She focused on that. She reminded Cricket of herself. How often things seemed unfair to her. Like she had fewer rights because she was a child.

"Has this happened before, in another store?" Officer Bryant asked.

"No!" Bunny said.

Richard put both arms around his wife and everyone else took a collective breath. The officers had pushed things further than Bunny's emotional legs could carry her. Cricket had never seen her mother look so upset about something—about something that Cricket actually understood. Usually her mother was furious about things that didn't make any sense, like mud on the bottom of your shoes tracked into the house or rings on the table because you didn't use a coaster. But hearing that your mother might have a serious illness, well, it made sense that that was upsetting. Cricket felt bad for her mother. She never felt bad for her mother.

"Shall we continue? You want to take a break?" Coolidge asked.

"Bun, you want to keep going?"

"Yes!" she said. "Let's just get this over with."

"Okay. In this case the store did not press charges. They took your mother's picture. It's on file and they'll watch out for her if she comes in again."

This part was news to Cricket. She wondered if they'd taken her picture as well.

"In the meantime," he continued, "they did exactly what they are supposed to do. They looked out for your daughter. Your daughter was a minor in the care of a somewhat incapacitated senior. In a situation like this, legally, they have two choices: turn your mother over to Adult Protective Services and give your daughter to Child Protective Services or turn them both over to police until a relative can be found."

"Protective Services? What for? I don't understand why they weren't allowed to go home."

The sergeant appeared with two bottles of cold water. Richard gladly took one and opened it for his wife.

"It's a lot to process. Your mother was showing signs of confusion. She wasn't displaying good judgment. She was responsible for a minor. They could have wandered off. They could have gotten lost. They could have been in danger. When this comes to our attention, we have to protect the child."

Cricket hadn't understood this until now. The police and the store had a legal responsibility. Her safety was considered a more pressing issue than Dodo's shoplifting.

The sergeant showed Bunny and Richard a wall of posters to the left of his desk. There were rows of faces. A number of the faces, he explained, belonged to missing persons who had Alzheimer's or dementia.

Cricket looked at the faces. Were they like Dodo? Was that what they were saying, that she was demented?

Poor Dodo. Cricket turned to her grandmother. Dodo's expression was impossible to read. She had crawled inside herself, like a turtle.

"Helping families find loved ones who have wandered off because of dementia, that is a lot of what we do. It's a national program. We found someone from Minnesota last week. We got him back to his family. Mrs. Cohen, the store did the right thing. They did the kind thing. Separating your mother and your daughter would have been quite traumatic."

"And rounding them up in a police car and taking them down to the precinct, that isn't traumatic?"

The sergeant handed Bunny the box of tissues.

"Bunny, try and calm down," Richard said. "No one's working against us here."

"Mrs. Cohen, you're very upset, it's understandable."

Bunny and Richard looked over at Dodo and Cricket. Part of Cricket wanted to run into their arms. The other part didn't want to leave Dodo alone.

"Mr. and Mrs. Cohen, these situations don't always end so peacefully," the sergeant said. "Confused elders are often agitated and disoriented. They lash out, they fight. This was like a dream version of what could have happened."

"Mr. and Mrs. Cohen, your mother is a very charismatic lady," said Bryant. "To be honest, myself and Officer Coolidge found it a privilege to escort her back here. But the real hero of the day is your daughter. You are very lucky."

Cricket couldn't believe what she'd just heard. She was actually pretty sure she'd imagined it.

"It's hard to see the silver lining here," Coolidge said. "But if there is one today, it's your daughter. She's got a real knack for following her grandmother's thinking and helping to reorient her. Without making her feel bad about her confusion. She has a very calming effect on Mrs. Fabricant. She talks to her with respect."

Dodo took Cricket's hand. Maybe she had been listening to everything.

"It's true," Bryant said. "The situation can be so frustrating because caregivers or relatives just can't deal with the senior's inability to remember the simplest things. So they get angry. Understandably. Alzheimer's is one of those diseases that affects the families just as much as, maybe more than, the person with the condition. But the more irritated the caregiver gets, the more disoriented and agitated the confused person gets, and it just feeds off itself."

Bunny was the one who was so impatient with Dodo. She was the one who got irritated. She was the one who'd moved her mother here, trying to keep her safe. And she was the one who just lost her patience more often than not. Cricket wondered if Bunny was beating herself up about everything.

"Keeping a person calm and relaxed is the best thing to do. The confused person is confused. It doesn't matter how many times you use rational thought, they will still be confused. But your daughter has a real gift. You're very lucky they were together. Your mother could have wound up somewhere very different than where she is now," Bryant said.

"If she were my daughter, I'd be very proud. You got a good girl there," the sergeant said.

Cricket was mildly insulted at being spoken about as though she weren't there, but she also wanted to roll over like a dog and have her tummy rubbed. She actually wanted to jump up. She wasn't simply an irresponsible maker-upper of tall tales anymore. According to the officers of New York's Nineteenth Precinct, Cricket Cohen was not bad. She was good. She had a gift. She was an asset to her family. This was what they were saying. Her parents had better remember.

"Thank you," Richard said. He looked over at Cricket. "Your ears must be burning. Everyone's talking about you. You okay, Dodo? Can we borrow Cricket?"

Dodo gave Cricket a little shove in the direction of her parents. They put their arms around her. Her mother kissed her over and over. Bunny had tears running down her cheeks that were now on Cricket's cheeks.

"Before we release them," Officer Bryant said, "we have to give you the following referrals. We highly recommend Mrs. Fabricant be evaluated for Alzheimer's. There are cognitive tests that her GP can run. The doctor can take it from there. And we are giving you this literature about a very good program that links all kinds of resources together to help families. Today ended well. Thank goodness. But you should prepare yourselves. Shoplifting is often one of the first things to happen in a longer list of typical behaviors. A lot of people wander at night. Does your mother live alone?" Bryant said.

"Mrs. Cohen," the sergeant asked, "how long has your mother been showing these symptoms?"

Bunny blinked like she was caught in a blizzard. Like the questions were coming at her so fast, and she couldn't see two inches in front of her. Bunny had always perceived Dodo as a nut, an eccentric, someone who got into fights with people about nothing. She was notorious. Was this not true? Cricket could tell that Bunny was asking herself if her mother was truly the victim of a brain that struggled against itself.

"Bun, how long do you think?"

"Forever?" Bunny said helplessly.

"At least a couple of years," Richard said.

"How long do you think, Cricket?" Bunny asked. It was the first time Cricket could remember her mother treating her like an adult.

"I think it's gotten worse since she moved to New York," Cricket said.

"I think that's right," Richard said. "She's been under a lot of stress. She retired, she moved. Bunny, she often doesn't know what day it is, she forgets the plan. But it's not the end of the world. The officers are right. We're very lucky something worse didn't happen."

"I don't feel lucky," Bunny said.

"We are lucky."

"How?"

"Like they could have ended up at Bellevue Hospital, honey, they could have lost each other at Grand Central Terminal, they could have been mugged, they could have gotten hurt. But everyone's safe and nothing bad happened."

"Richard, my mother was caught shoplifting! That is not nothing."

"Bun, it isn't anything to be ashamed of."

"I'm ashamed," Bunny said. "I've been so hard on her. I've been so hard on everyone. I'm so ashamed." Bunny burst into tears and apologized and couldn't stop apologizing.

30

BREADSTICKS AND MARBLES

t was five-thirty when the Cohens and Dodo walked out of the Nineteenth Precinct. Cricket felt like it had been a lifetime since she'd seen the light for real, not through a window.

"I could eat a horse," Bunny said. "Richard, did we have lunch today?"

"No," he said.

"Let's treat ourselves to Gino's. We can't afford it, but we deserve it."

"I can afford it," Dodo said. "I'll take us. We all deserve something very pampering."

Bunny linked arms with Cricket, who linked arms with Dodo, who was escorted on the other side by Richard. They walked like that, taking up the whole sidewalk. Bunny was giddy and Cricket felt like she was living in two worlds at the same time. She was determined to remember, for the rest of her life if possible, what this was like—a moment when her mother wasn't worried or angry about something. Cricket was also trying to commit to memory what had happened in the police station. She felt she might need to recall it. Her mother had asked her opinion. Like Cricket was an expert. Like Cricket's opinion mattered. Her mother had cried on her shoulder. Her mother had thanked her.

Occasionally, because they were taking up most of the sidewalk, the Cohen group had to split up to let other people pass. But even then, Bunny didn't let go of Cricket.

Gino's had yellow-and-black zebra wallpaper inside. When Richard was still a partner at the law firm, they used to come here. It had been a long time. They rarely came anymore. Cricket was happy to be back. What a day. In a way she had had the truest adventure of her whole life and it was ending with a bang, in a fantastic restaurant. A waiter appeared from nowhere and pushed Cricket's chair with Cricket sitting on it in to the table.

He did the same for Dodo, and she laughed because she said she felt like a kid on a ride.

He brought a bottle of wine, and a soda for Cricket.

"Here's to Cricket," Bunny said.

"Here's to Cricket," Richard said.

"Hear, hear. To Cricket," Dodo said.

Everyone clinked glasses. "To my unsung hero," Bunny said. "Thank you, Cricket."

"For what?" Cricket asked. *Hero* wasn't a word she'd ever expected to hear her parents use to describe her. But nothing today had gone like she'd expected.

"For being you," Bunny said. "For being my daughter. You possess everything I lack. It is infuriating sometimes. But thank goodness you are you."

Richard put his arm around his daughter.

Was this a dream? The waiter came by with breadsticks. The breadsticks were real.

Bunny grabbed one and said, "God bless gluten."

"God bless gluten," Richard said, too.

"So," Dodo said, after a big guzzle of wine, "let's get to business. Have I lost my marbles? Is that the consensus?"

Aha, Dodo had been paying attention to everything. She may have crawled inside her shell like a turtle at the police precinct, but she had stereophonic sound in there. Bunny burst out laughing.

"Mother, do you think you've lost your marbles?"

"Not yet. Not entirely. But they're definitely rattling around in there. I looked up Alzheimer's a few years ago. I noticed I was forgetting where I put things. Apparently I can have it for a long time before I need to make any changes."

Bunny and Richard sipped their wine. They gave each other a long look.

Dodo said, "I will agree to let you hire someone. I will allow you to hire someone to make sure I don't steal things or set myself on fire. But I don't plan on talking with them. Or liking them. And please, for my sake, buy them a cookbook."

Their salads arrived, along with a giant plate of delicately fried zucchini and its blossoms. Cricket almost asked for ketchup (just to be funny), but she didn't.

"You know what, let's just get through the summer, Mother. Come to the Hamptons with us. We'll all be together and we'll find a doctor out there to get an assessment. How does that sound?"

"So reasonable," Richard said.

"Really, really reasonable," Cricket agreed. "Are you okay, Mom?"

"Wait, you're telling me that I'm not usually this reasonable? Don't answer." Bunny ran her hands through her hair and took a deep breath. "I'm apologizing to everyone. Especially to you, Mother. I've been mad at you. But this isn't your fault. It's my fault. I didn't want to know. I've been in denial. I guess because I want you to be my mother the way I remember. I don't want you to change."

"Me neither, Bunny. If it makes you feel better, me neither," Dodo said. "I guess we're all good at pretending." She squeezed Cricket's hand under the table.

"What did Marvin Morgan always say, Cricket, about denial?" Richard asked.

"It's not just a river in Egypt," Cricket said.

"Who is Marvin Morgan? He's very funny," Dodo said.

"He's a psychiatrist, the father of a friend of Cricket's," Richard said. "Veronica Morgan's father."

"I always liked that Veronica girl," her grandmother said.

"Me, too," Cricket said. "Her father also said that denial was one of the most underrated coping mechanisms known to mankind."

"That's right, and I used to think he was kidding. But maybe not," Bunny said. "Anyway, I'm not kidding about how good this antipasto is. Or how much I want to get home."

"Me, too," said Richard.

"Maybe we can watch a movie together tonight," suggested Cricket. "Something with Bette Davis."

"That sounds lovely," Dodo said. "But first, Cricket and I have to check out of our room at the Pierre."

Bunny laughed. "Oh, Mother. I think you're imagining—"

"She's not, Mom," said Cricket.

"I beg your pardon?" Bunny said.

"Cricket and I had—what would you call it, Cricket?" Dodo asked.

"I would call it an adventure, Dodo."

The waiter came just in time and refilled Bunny's wineglass.

"What do you mean, Cricket?" her father asked. "Something else happened before Barneys and the police station?"

She looked at Dodo and they both smiled.

"Yes," Cricket said. The time had come to confess that part of their adventure.

31

"THE ERRATICS OF WEST SIXTY-FOURTH STREET"

by Cricket Cohen

Memoir Project

Mr. Ludgate

As long as I can remember, my grandmother and I have been really good at pretending. We've been contestants on game shows, we had our own cooking network. We've pretended to be explorers on other planets, immigrants from foreign countries who didn't speak English, blind people who had to understand the world with their fingers. We have a lot in common, my grandmother and I, even though she is seventy-five and

I am eleven. A few days ago we ran away. I'm tempted to tell you that when we ran away we boarded a steamship filled with international spies, that we avoided deadly run-ins with evil dictators, and that my grandmother stole a diamond the size of a grapefruit.

But the truth is, we just walked across Central Park to the Upper East Side of Manhattan. Central Park is full of erratics. You've probably seen them, gigantic boulders that sit on top of landscapes they don't belong in. A long time ago, glaciers pushed them here from far away. My grandmother is an erratic. She was pushed here from another place by a force more powerful than herself—my mother.

During our walk, a man on roller skates crashed into us. We almost died. I thought that was the story I'd tell everyone about. Little did I know.

Later, we checked into a hotel and spent the night. The hotel was so fancy it had four different kinds of showerheads. I thought that was the story I'd tell everyone. Little did I know.

We went to Barneys and my grandmother took a shawl. It turns out she may be in the early stages of Alzheimer's disease. She is going for tests soon. She repeats a lot of things. She gets confused. Sometimes she sees things that aren't there. She's mad that people

don't want her to fight back. I think she's mad that
people treat her like an old person. I think she took the
shawl because she's mad about losing her purpose.
Even if she is losing her memory, she isn't losing her
personality. She shouldn't have to lose her dignity.
But I guess lots of people don't like old people. At least
that's what she says. But I love her. I can't imagine not
loving her.

Men in suits wanted the shawl back, so they took us
in a padded elevator to the basement, and then they
sent us away with the police. I thought we'd be sent to
prison. I wasn't sure my family would try to get me
back, and if that was the story, I didn't think it was one
I could ever tell anyone. I hadn't done what they
wanted me to. I mean I did do it—they wanted me to
write this memoir—but I didn't write it when they told
me to write it. They don't like when I don't do the
things they want me to do at the exact time that they
want me to do them. I think there are a lot of things in
my grandmother's life that she doesn't like either. So
she tries to rearrange them. People call that lying. I
think lying is when you say something untrue to cause
pain or get someone in trouble. I don't do that. Neither
does my grandmother.

Here's what else I think. People absorb pressure.

Memories and experiences seep into brains like water seeps into rocks. Over time, your experiences and your memories expand and contract, causing erosion. Maybe that's what Alzheimer's disease is.

My grandmother misses my grandfather. Sometimes I see her looking lost and I'm pretty sure she's thinking about him.

If you pay attention, a person will give you clues about themselves, just like a rock. And maybe life is like that, too. At first I didn't understand why I had to rewrite my memoir. People (aka Mr. Ludgate and my parents) thought that my made-up stories got in the way of my real story. I guess there is truth to that. I didn't make this memoir up at all. I just thought about the truth of my grandmother. I thought about what she means to me and I wrote it down.

ACKNOWLEDGMENTS

The real-life inspiration for Cricket's favorite scientist, Dr. T, is Dr. G, also known as Dr. Laura Guertin. Her blog (journeysofdrg .org) lit up my imagination. I was very fortunate that she agreed to read over the geology sections of this book. I still can't believe that she corresponded with me and tried to help me. Stephen Porder of Brown University was also generous in this way. They were like private professors. I'm obviously not a scientist, though, and any errors are mine alone. Steven Kidder of CUNY and Diana Marsh are also scientists who let me, a non-scientist ignoramus, bounce ideas off them. David Shenk is a writer I met at a birthday party. While eating cake, he let me describe an idea I had about the relationship of pressure in geology to memory loss in people. Wesley Adams gave me loads of wonderful ideas and encouragement. I'm eternally grateful to FSG's copy editors, too. Adam Forgash, Paul Bravmann, Sarah Burnes, and Logan Garrison Savits read drafts and gave me valuable feedback. If these generous and smart people hadn't lent me their time and their ears and their thoughts, I'd still be sitting around procrastinating, imagining a story about a curious girl and her declining but wonderful grandmother.